Cross the Line

Editing by One Love Editing

Proofreading by Sid Damiano

Cover illustration by Seaj Art

Becca Steele

www.authorbeccasteele.com

CROSS THE LINE

USA TODAY & *WALL STREET JOURNAL* BESTSELLING AUTHOR

BECCA STEELE

AUTHOR'S NOTE

The author is British, and British English spellings are used throughout.

For Si & Jon

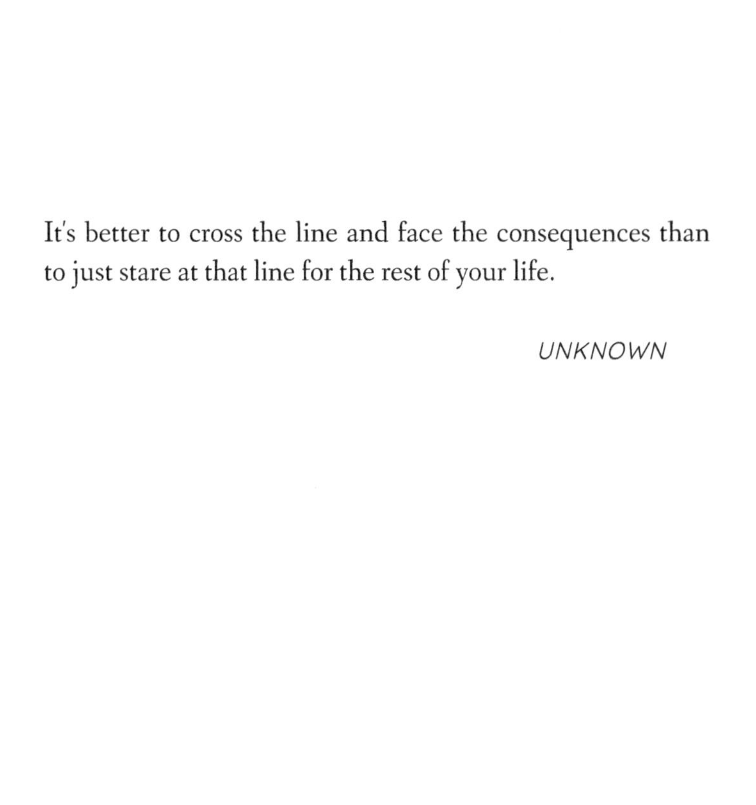

It's better to cross the line and face the consequences than to just stare at that line for the rest of your life.

UNKNOWN

PRESTON

HALLOWEEN

Flicking the switch on my mask's LED lights to turn them off, I melted deep into the shadows of the haunted house, undetected, watching *him* sneak up behind a girl.

She screamed in terror, struggling against his body. Hot jealousy burned through my veins, and I gritted my teeth, forcing myself not to react as my teammate-slash-antagonist murmured something to the girl before lifting his mask, running his lips over the exposed skin of her neck.

The corridor echoed with the pounding of heavy footsteps, and Carter came up behind him, ripping him away from the girl and simultaneously giving him a shove, in the direction of my hiding place. I heard him snarl, "You're not playing fair," before Carter and the girl disappeared.

I acted on instinct, before I could think it through. Leaping out of the shadows, I threw my body against his, sending us both staggering back against the wall. His mask was still raised, pushed up on the top of his head, and I tore off my own, before bringing my lips to his ear.

"Hello, Kian."

His whole body stiffened, and I heard his breathing quicken as I ran my nose down his jaw.

When he spoke, he only said one word, but his voice came out as a low, tortured scrape that had my cock stiffening in my jeans.

"Preston."

ONE

KIAN

SEPTEMBER

"You're off the team."

At those four words, I saw red.

"*Fuck*!" Flying out of my chair, I spun and threw it across the room, sending it crashing into the wall. "Fuck!"

"Mate, calm down." Carter Blackthorne, Alstone High's football team captain and my best friend, grabbed me in a hold, pinning my arms.

"I'll ignore your little temper tantrum," Mr. Anders, our football coach, commented dryly. "What did you think would happen? You were irresponsible enough to bring drugs onto school premises, therefore you have to face the consequences." He continued as if I wasn't raging, Carter the only thing stopping me from tearing up his office. "You're lucky it's only a suspension. Professor Sharpe wanted you permanently kicked off the team, but I managed to talk him out of it. If you can behave, you'll be allowed back. That means no more trouble while you're in the vicinity of Alstone High. I don't care what you do in your own time, but when you're here, you behave. Do I make myself clear?"

"Yes." I spat the word through gritted teeth. *Shit.* There was barely any weed in my locker; it was only supposed to be enough to get Professor Sharpe, Alstone High's headmaster, to call my parents. Maybe a week or two of detention. Being kicked off the football team and being stopped from doing the only thing I was any good at...that hadn't even featured on my radar.

Carter released his grip, and I spun towards the door. "You're suspended from school for a week, as well," Mr. Anders called after me.

I slammed my fist into his filing cabinet, welcoming the jarring pain that raced up my arm.

Could this day get any worse?

Carter caught up with me as I was stalking across the football pitch. "Kian? What the fuck's going on with you?"

Sinking onto the bench at the side of the pitch, I put my head in my hands. "I fucked up, alright? What do you want me to say?"

Next to me, I heard his heavy sigh as he took a seat. "They're not worth jeopardising your future for. Now we've lost our star player. What are we supposed to do?"

"I don't know," I muttered. Lifting my head, I stared at my best friend. "I'm sorry."

He studied me for a moment, concern clear in his gaze, before he clapped me on the shoulder. "Lucky for you, Coach gave me a heads-up, and he thinks he's found a solution in the meantime while we wait for your return. He'd better be as good as they say, otherwise we really will be screwed."

"What's that supposed to mean?"

"You know the new boy? Preston?"

"The American?" Yeah, I knew who he was. *Preston Montgomery III*. Hard to miss him, really, when half of the girls at school had been panting over him ever since the first day he'd shown up.

He nodded. "Yeah, that's him. He was on the football team back in his previous school. The coach has seen video footage of him playing, and he said he's really talented." His gaze turned to the pitch, looking towards the football goal. "He's a striker. I've invited him to try out for the team. Today."

"So I get suspended from school, kicked off the team, and replaced, all in one afternoon? Well, today fucking sucks."

"You're not being replaced. What else am I meant to do, Kian? There's no one else that's anywhere near your skill level." He climbed to his feet as a blond figure came into view at the far end of the pitch. "Be nice," he warned me, leaving me to sulk on the benches as he jogged over to greet Preston. I watched as they fell into discussion, Carter gesturing towards the goal and the pitch every now and then.

The rest of the team came filing out of the gym changing rooms, and I steeled myself for the comments I knew were coming my way. I deserved them. This was our final year at Alstone High, one final chance to prove ourselves as football legends before we left for university. Being kicked off the team might have cost us our chance.

"Before you all say it..." I got to my feet as the team neared me. "Yes, I messed up, but you—we're a team. I'm only one player."

"Our best player." Chris, one of our defenders, gave me a pointed look.

"Maybe some of you lazy bastards will actually put

some work in now." I clenched my jaw, staring him down until he dropped his gaze.

"Alright, break it up." Carter moved to the front of the cluster of players standing around me. Lifting his hand, he waved it in the direction of Preston. "Everyone, this is Preston. He's trying out for the team today, so let's put him through his paces. Don't go easy on him." He grinned.

A smugly confident smile spread across Preston's face. "Show me what you've got."

After the warm-up, the team moved into formation. From the second Preston touched the ball, I couldn't tear my gaze away. His strong, muscular legs moved the ball effortlessly down the field, easily bypassing the defence. I could see him instantly calculating his chances, and he took the tiny opening between two players, gracefully flicking the ball to send it curving past the goalie and into the corner of the net.

Pure fucking poetry in motion.

"Kian who?" Chris shouted to me as the coach blew the whistle, slapping Preston's hand in congratulations as he passed him.

In that moment, I hated Preston Montgomery III.

After practice was over, Carter gathered the team together to vote. It was only a formality—no one could deny Preston's skill, plus, the coach had the final say. The vote was unanimous, the whole team fawning over the golden boy, showering him in praise.

As everyone made their way off the field, on a high, I remained where I was. Slumped on the bench, head in my hands, I was forgotten.

"Kian?"

"What do you want?" I sprung to my feet, making Preston stumble backwards in shock. "Come to gloat?"

"No." His stupid perfect mouth turned down, his brows pulling together. "I thought I'd come and see if you were okay. You know, after everything."

"Why would you care? We're not friends. You've taken my place on the team—congratulations. Now, get out of my face."

"Hey, no hard feelings, man. Carter asked me to step in, so I did. The team needs me until you're back from your suspension." He eyed me warily.

"What do you want, a medal? So you had a good game, so what. I'm not interested in talking to you."

His eyes hardened, the light going out of them. "Fine. If that's how you want to be."

"It is."

"Okay." His nostrils flared, and his jaw set. "Don't mistake me for an easy target you can push around."

"Don't mistake me for someone who gives a shit about your feelings. Stay out of my way."

A low, rumbling growl came from his throat, but he clamped his mouth shut. Without another word, he dismissed me by turning his back, stalking away in harsh, angry strides.

Every football practice, I was there, watching from the sidelines, Preston always commanding my entire focus. Torturing myself with the knowledge that I'd been replaced by someone who was easily as good as me, if not better.

Every day, I resented him a little more.

Every day, he burrowed deeper under my skin.

TWO

PRESTON

OCTOBER

"Great job. I had every faith in you, son." Coach clapped me on the back as I came to a halt at the edge of the field, wiping the sweat from my brows. A huge grin spread across my face. I was an outsider in this place, but here on the field, I belonged. Scoring three goals, winning the praise of my teammates? Nothing could beat that.

"Not bad, mate." Carter, soccer team captain and midfielder, held out his hand for a fist bump, which I accepted. The smile remained on my face as he jogged away in the direction of the locker room with the rest of my teammates, their congratulations leaving me on a high.

Heading over to the side of the field, I swiped a bottle of water from the pile resting on the table, uncapped it, and lifted it to my mouth—then paused, the bottle halfway to my lips.

Kian Courtland, legendary striker, currently suspended

from the team, was watching me from the sidelines with a dark, angry glare in his pale green eyes.

Guess he was still pissed that I was the one getting the praise. It was his own fault he'd managed to get himself suspended from the team. Being caught with weed in his locker? Yeah, he deserved it. I raised a brow, taunting him, and his gaze narrowed, his fists clenching, probably imagining his hands around my throat.

My cock stirred in my shorts, and I groaned. *Not again.* It was difficult enough being the new guy at Alstone High, let alone an American in a foreign country. Add being gay and attracted to someone who was not only harbouring a grudge against me, but was decidedly straight based on the girls he always surrounded himself with?

It sucked.

What was it about him? He was my opposite in every way. Black dishevelled hair to my perfectly coiffed blond, lean to my bulkier build, and an abrasive attitude to my generally easy-going nature. And his lip piercing. Couldn't forget that. The only thing we had in common was our skill on the soccer field.

Fuck. He was coming over.

"Think you're fucking special, do ya, Golden Boy?" He came to a stop in front of me, hostility radiating off him as he stood, arms crossed, shooting daggers from his eyes.

I rolled my eyes at his juvenile nickname for me. "I know I'm special. What was the view like from the sidelines, Delinquent?"

A muscle ticked in his jaw as he took a threatening step towards me. "I told you to never use that word in relation to me again. And fuck you. You're just the shiny new toy. When I'm back, I'll be the leading goal scorer again, the team MVP."

I let my gaze bore into his, not backing down. Give someone like Kian an inch, and they'd take a mile. We were nose to nose, both more or less the same height, which I was grateful for because it meant he couldn't use his height to intimidate me. "Stop referring to me as Golden Boy and I might consider it."

"Do I look like I take orders from you?" He bristled, shoving against my chest. "Get out of my face."

"You're the one in my face," I commented mildly, which caused him to bare his teeth in a snarl. My gaze dropped to his lips, his piercing glinting in the sun. Man, I wanted to run my tongue over that piercing. I licked my lips, and his eyes darkened as they followed the movement of my tongue. The tension between us crackled with energy, morphing from hostile to...something else.

Then, he shoved against my chest again and I stumbled backwards, taken off guard. He let out a low, taunting chuckle, elbowing past me and stalking off the field.

Back at the house, I dropped my bags by the front door and followed the smell of baking into the kitchen to find my mom in the middle of transferring a tray of cookies, fresh from the oven, onto a cooling rack.

"Just in time." I grinned, swooping in on the rack.

My mom batted my hand away. "Not yet, you'll burn your mouth. Have patience." She softened her words with a smile as she looked at me. "How was practice?"

"Good." I returned her smile. As usual, she looked completely put together, all blonde elegance—the perfect

Stepford wife at first glance, although she was anything but subservient. She and my dad made a great team, and I was lucky to have them as parents.

"Your father will be home late tonight; he's caught up at work." Untying her apron, she hung it on a hook on the back of the door, then began pulling pans from the cupboards.

I nodded. My dad's role as a financial analyst often had him working long hours. He'd been handpicked by his US-based employers to move to London, as part of a small team heading up the new branch they'd opened up over the summer. Used to being on the coast, none of us had wanted to live in London, so we'd ended up here in Alstone. From what I'd seen of it so far, it was okay, other than the fact that everything was so fucking small compared to what we were used to. Roads, houses, cars... Still, I guess it made sense, since we were on a tiny island. I missed the US—the feeling of space, my old home near the beach in Stamford, Connecticut, and my school. Most of all, though, I missed my group of friends—their casual acceptance of my being openly gay, and the way we all looked out for one another.

I'd spent my eighteenth birthday here alone, since it had taken place before I'd started at Alstone High, and I didn't yet know anyone. That had been a low point for me, but things had improved since then. Thanks to my soccer skills, I'd quickly become popular in school, although I still felt like the new guy, the outsider. Hence the fact I hadn't yet broadcast my sexual orientation. I wasn't ashamed, and I wasn't about to deny it if I was asked, but I guess the move overseas had left me unsure about my place in this new world. I wanted to be more settled before I announced it.

I'd been lucky in the past, but my ex-boyfriend, Blake, had gone to a different school...and let's just say that a broken arm was the least of his problems when he'd come out in front of the entire football team.

I sighed. I needed to give it time. Moving to a new house was stressful enough, and I'd moved halfway across the world. I couldn't expect everything to fall into place straight away.

My mom interrupted my melancholy thoughts, sliding a plate in front of me. Thanking her, I took the plate and headed up to my room.

After I'd demolished the cookies, I lay on my bed, thinking back to today's soccer practice, and the heat of Kian's body pressed against mine as we stared each other down.

My dick reacted like it always did when I thought of him, and I forced myself to focus on soccer formations in my head, pushing him out of my mind.

Pale green eyes invaded my thoughts again, and I groaned aloud.

Time to try something else. I mentally began listing his negative points.

Arrogant.
Rude.
Abrasive.
Troublemaker.
Delinquent.
Straight (99% sure).
Hates me.

Halfway through, things somehow changed.

Green eyes I want to get lost in.

Lip piercing.
Chiselled jaw.
Hot. Fucking hot.
Mine.

I was so fucking screwed.

THREE

PRESTON

Carter Blackthorne, Xavier Wright, and Kian Courtland. I looked up, my gaze drawn to the three kings of Alstone High as they strolled towards us with their typical casual, confident swagger. Kian pulled out a chair and sprawled in it, no care in the world as he stared at the people flocking around him with disinterest. It was like they were flies, buzzing around him, and yet he couldn't be bothered to swat them away.

I cleared my throat, acting like I didn't notice the scowl he was directing my way, and turned my attention to the conversation about our upcoming game against Highnam Academy. After reassuring the guys that I had it all under control, never mind the fact I had no idea what Highnam Academy were like as a team, we discussed tactics for the upcoming game. Eventually, Kian's dirty looks got too pointed to ignore, and I got to my feet, stretching out my whole body. I didn't miss the way his eyes honed straight in on the strip of skin that was exposed when I lifted my arms, my untucked shirt riding up. Was I imagining the flash of heat in his eyes? Probably.

"Ah, put them away, mate." The playful tease came from Chris, one of my teammates, and I smirked.

"You don't wanna see these muscles?" I purposely lifted my shirt higher, flexing my abs. Groans echoed around the table, except for one person who was noticeably silent.

Kian.

Now I was positive I wasn't imagining the heat in his gaze as he stared at me.

It was too much. After tucking my shirt back in and straightening my school blazer, I swung my bag over my shoulder. "Catch ya later."

I sauntered away from the table and back into the main school building, deceptively casual, but my legs were threatening to give way.

Fucking Kian Courtland.

Where to go? The bathrooms were too busy; I needed to be alone. Switching direction at the last minute, I headed down the corridor and through the double doors that led outside to the gym and locker rooms that were used exclusively by the sports teams.

I used my pass to enter the silent building. If I'd been here ten minutes earlier, it probably would've been teeming with school athletes, but right now, towards the end of lunch period, most had disappeared to get sustenance before the afternoon.

Making my way into the locker room, I lowered my bag to the floor and sank down onto one of the wooden benches in front of the bank of lockers, placing my head in my hands.

I don't know how long I sat there, just breathing in and out, but eventually I became aware of a presence in the room. I lowered my hands and turned my head, already knowing who I'd see.

Kian.

Staring down at me with arrogant contempt, hot and brooding, he was a dark prince, and I was his subject.

No. I needed to remind him, and myself, that we were equals. He may have been top of the food chain, but that didn't give him the right to lord it over me. Jumping up so fast that I almost made myself dizzy, I moved to lean against the lockers, the bench between us giving me some breathing room.

The air surrounding us thickened, my traitorous cock stirring as our eyes locked and I took in the dark expression on his face. Fuck. I hoped he didn't notice.

He rounded the bench, coming to a stop a few feet away from me.

"What's your deal, Golden Boy? Trying to take my place? Worm your way in with my friends? Remember, you're new, and I've paid my dues. Don't even fucking dream of trying to replace me."

"I'm not trying to cause trouble," I told him honestly.

His lip curled, and he took a threatening step closer. "Stop trying to take my fucking place, then. If you do, you'll regret it."

"Really? Want to bet on that? Seems like your friends like me. Coach likes me. He told me I was integral to the team," I goaded. "Everyone's replaceable. Even the mighty Kian Courtland." I needed to stop provoking him, but he riled me up and I couldn't seem to help running my mouth whenever he confronted me.

For the first time, a flicker of uncertainty appeared in his eyes, and I was struck with a pang of regret. "Hey, I didn't mean—"

He interrupted me. "Why are you looking at me like that? Are you gay or something?"

His low question seemed to echo all around us, and I swallowed nervously. Now was the moment of truth.

"Yes, I am."

There was complete silence in the room. He just stared at me, sucking his bottom lip into his mouth and worrying at his lip ring. Making a snap decision, that I hoped wouldn't end up with me getting sucker punched, *again*, I stepped closer than I'd ever dared before. Our bodies were touching now, my cock abrading against his thigh as he shifted position, trying for nonchalance even though there was a raging inferno swallowing us whole. Inclining my head, I lowered my voice to speak in his ear, attempting to keep my tone controlled. "Are you?"

"No." His emphatic denial came out far too quickly, but he hadn't moved from his spot, and as I pressed my hips to his, the layers of material between us did nothing to conceal the rigidness of his cock against my own.

I smiled, dipping my head to his neck and inhaling the subtle, heady spice of his addictive scent. "Could've fooled me," I murmured.

"I fucking hate you. You're nothing to me. *Nothing*."

Yet still, he didn't move.

"Is that so? Why aren't you moving, then? Anyone could come in here and catch us like this."

My words suddenly jolted him into action, and he pushed at my chest so hard, I staggered backwards, crashing into the bank of lockers.

"Stay the fuck away from me." He stalked off towards the doors, wrenching them open and disappearing from the room.

I straightened up with a sigh, rubbing at the back of my head where it had slammed into the locker. I'd pushed him too far, and now he was gone.

One thing I knew for sure now, though, was that Kian wanted me—even though he didn't *want* to want me.

That, I could work with.

FOUR

PRESTON

HALLOWEEN

I took the mask Xavier handed to me, slipping it over my face and flicking the switch to activate the lights. Everything was suddenly bathed in a yellow glow, and I held up my phone to take a selfie.

I chuckled at the image. Neon yellow slashes in the shape of an X covered both eye areas, and the mouth was outlined in yet more slashes, approximating a huge, sinister grin. After uploading the image to my social media so my friends back home could see it, I pulled my hood on top of my head and melted into the crowd of guys.

Initially, I'd been a little disappointed when Alstone High hadn't seemed to be planning anything for Halloween. Back at home in the US, my whole school would've been celebrating, and the entire neighbourhood would have gone all out with decorations. Here, everything seemed disappointingly low-key in comparison.

Now, though, standing around the back of the haunted house with the sounds of the county council-organised

Fright Night carnival echoing through the evening air, things were looking up. I half listened as Carter began barking out instructions, my eyes constantly straying to the guy in the red mask standing to his right.

Kian.

We'd avoided each other for the rest of the week at school. Yeah, we'd ended up sitting at the same table at lunch, and we'd shared some of the same classes, but neither of us had spoken. I'd caught him watching me, though, his gaze always dark and contemptuous, but there was a heat to it that hadn't been there before.

Carter reeled off a list of dos and don'ts relating to some shit involving capturing girls, but since I wasn't going to be doing that, I didn't pay attention. Instead, I remained fixated on Kian. As if he was aware of my scrutiny, he turned his head in my direction.

I sucked in a breath as the group of guys began moving towards the front of the haunted house, headed up by Carter, Xavier, and Kian. When Kian drew level with me, he paused for a moment, his voice a taunting drawl. "A yellow mask for the golden boy. Appropriate. Shame you have to sit this little game out, huh?"

Leaning closer, I whispered my words for his ears only. "Maybe I'll take part in the chase. Maybe I'll catch myself a delinquent."

"Don't even fucking think about it," he growled, shouldering past me.

A grin spread across my face. Man, he was so easy to rile up. He dished it out, and I gave it right back. There was something about getting under his skin that was so damn satisfying.

The sound of the siren from *The Purge* reverberated around the park, and I waited until the echoes died away before making my own way around to the front of the haunted house.

Illuminated by the sweeping coloured lights, I watched the guys in their neon LED masks dart between stalls and rides in pursuit of their prey. Shaking my head, I turned in the direction of the haunted house, passing through the gaping mouth and into the darkness inside.

A guy dressed as a clown with a white painted face and distorted, bloody grin ran at me, but I sidestepped him, continuing through the corridors. Rounding a corner, I found myself in a dimly-lit open space, with a cackling witch who was stirring a cauldron.

She called out to me in a low, croaking voice, but my attention was diverted. Out of the corner of my eye I saw a flash of red, and I paused, switching direction and heading down the corridor to my left.

Flicking the switch on my mask's LED lights to turn them off, I melted deep into the shadows of the haunted house, undetected, watching *him* sneak up behind a girl.

She screamed in terror, struggling against his body. Hot jealousy burned through my veins, and I gritted my teeth, forcing myself not to react as my teammate-slash-antagonist murmured something to the girl before lifting his mask, running his lips over the exposed skin of her neck.

The corridor echoed with the pounding of heavy footsteps, and Carter came up behind him, ripping him away from the girl and simultaneously giving him a shove, in the direction of my hiding place. I heard him snarl, "You're not playing fair," before Carter and the girl disappeared.

I acted on instinct, before I could think it through. Leaping out of the shadows, I threw my body against his, sending us both staggering back against the wall. His mask was still raised, pushed up on the top of his head, and I tore off my own, before bringing my lips to his ear.

"Hello, Kian."

His whole body stiffened, and I heard his breathing quicken as I ran my nose down his jaw.

When he spoke, he only said one word, but his voice came out as a low, tortured scrape that had my cock stiffening in my jeans.

"Preston."

KIAN

Fuck. One minute, I'd had a hot little female body pressed against me, all lush, soft curves and full tits, and the next, she was gone, and I was being pinned against the wall by six foot two of blond, all-American masculinity. Instead of softness, everything was hard. So fucking hard.

Preston brought his mouth back to my ear. I was frozen in place, just like before, when we'd been in almost this exact position in the changing rooms. "What do you want?" His voice was a sultry drawl that made my dick jump.

I pulled my lip between my teeth, concentrating on the bite of enamel against metal and skin, instead of the way he was grinding his hips slowly against mine.

"What do you want?" he repeated, his breaths getting harsher as he kept up his movements, and my dick lengthened, the tortuous pleasure of the friction against my jeans making me want to thrust my own hips into his. I fisted my hands at my sides, to stop myself from doing something I'd regret, like touch him.

I wasn't gay. I liked girls.

I didn't like guys. *Most of the time.*

Especially not ridiculously good-looking, mouthy American guys who were trying to take my position.

Without that position I was *nothing.*

With that thought, I finally got the strength to shove him away from me. "I want you to leave me alone." Trying to storm away with a raging boner was a lot more difficult than you'd think, and my mood soured as I stalked past the huge, neon Ferris wheel, towards the park gates.

The combination of the throbbing beat of the music playing from the sound system and the bright strobe lights flashing around me made my head pound. Forget picking up a girl—I wasn't in the mood anymore. It was time to move on to my next task of the evening, before I headed to the cove.

A hand gripping my bicep halted my trajectory, and I spun around to see Preston eyeing me with what looked like either apprehension or remorse on his pretty-boy face.

"I thought I told you to leave me alone." I bared my teeth at him.

"I wanted to apologise." He shrugged, his shoulders slumping. "I know I was out of line. It won't happen again."

Why the fuck did I feel a sense of disappointment at his words?

Raising my eyes to his, I studied him for a moment, pulling my lip between my teeth, before I gave up and allowed the words to come out. "You wanna be a delinquent for the night, Golden Boy? Put your mask back on, and follow me."

FIVE

PRESTON

"Where are we going?" Sliding into the passenger seat of Kian's car, I glanced over at him. His mask was still pushed up on the top of his head, and his eyes were sparking with wicked intention.

"Be quiet and let me drive." He started the engine, the car roaring to life with a growl. He changed gears with smooth, confident movements, the car picking up speed as we moved along the road.

"Damn, you look hot when you're driving," I muttered, immediately regretting the words. "Sorry."

His gaze swung to mine, his eyes bright in the glow of the streetlights. Surprisingly, he didn't comment. When I thought back to what had happened in the haunted house, I was shocked he'd even invited me to come with him.

"I've never driven stick before." I filled the uncomfortable silence with the first comment that came into my head. Kian's eyes were back on the road, but I saw them widen.

"Never?" His hands flexed on the steering wheel as we took a left onto a street lined with trees on one side, and a high stone wall on the other.

"Never."

"We need to rectify that," he said decisively.

"*We* do? Are we friends now?"

His eyes narrowed. "Does anything about any of our interactions so far make you think we are?"

A memory flashed through my mind.

I was on a high. First game after Kian Courtland, the star striker, had been suspended, and I'd managed to score four goals and an assist, leading us to a 5-1 win which put us in position at the top of the league table. It had taken me forever to escape afterwards—everyone wanted to congratulate me. Phrases like "Midas touch," "golden boy," and "star player" had all been banded around, and the attention was overwhelming. In the best way.

After opening the trunk of my car and placing my gym bag inside, I straightened up and turned around, realising I wasn't alone. Kian stood there, hard and threatening, lip curled and his pale green eyes glinting with anger.

"Golden Boy."

He spat the words at me. I opened my mouth to reply, but he hadn't finished. "Don't get any ideas about taking my place as the star player."

"Feeling threatened? Maybe you shouldn't have brought drugs into the school, Delinquent."

He snarled, and then without any warning, struck at me with a jab straight to the stomach.

Gasping, I doubled over in pain, tears coming to my eyes. I was dimly aware of him stalking away as I collapsed against my car.

Returning to the present, I shook my head. "Nope." Then I added, "What about now?"

"We're not friends." His jaw tightened, and I rolled my eyes. This guy was throwing out so many mixed signals that I'd be surprised if he even knew what was going on inside his head. Giving up for now, I turned away from him to stare out of the window instead.

Kian slowed the car as we came to a quiet, tree-lined street with widely spaced-out houses, Scandinavian-style with timber frames and huge glass windows. He pulled off the road next to a small clump of tall pine trees and turned to me. "You can wait here if you want."

"Why? What's going on?"

He didn't answer me. "Wonder if I'll get arrested, this time." There was a faraway look in his eyes, the hardness disappearing, replaced by an almost wistful look.

Unease settled heavy in my stomach, and my decision was simple.

"I'm coming."

"Mask on and hood up. And don't say a fucking word." He slid his mask into place, and I followed suit, exiting the car. I watched as he ducked back inside, pulling something from the back seat, and then he was jogging along the road and turning down one of the driveways leading to the sprawling houses. This house was dark and silent, not even a single Halloween decoration outside.

A beep sounded, and the garage door rolled up, smoothly and silently.

"Whose house is this?" I hissed.

"Mine. Stop fucking talking."

At his harsh whisper, I clamped my mouth shut. My questions would have to wait.

He headed inside the garage with long purposeful strides, swinging the baseball bat from his fingertips. Not pausing in his stride, he reached out and slammed his hand over a button on the wall and the door rolled back into place as the overhead lights automatically flickered on.

I stared around me. This place was like a car showroom. Gleaming metal machines sat in neat rows. There had to be at least twenty cars in here, all the same shade of polished silver.

I raised a brow. Weird, but whatever.

A loud crash echoed through the cavernous space, and I watched in horror as Kian swung the bat right at the centre of the windshield of the car in front of him. The car alarm began blaring as he struck it again and again, spiderwebs spreading across the glass. He then turned his attention to the hood, bringing the bat down with a shout of rage.

I finally took action, running up to him and ripping the bat from his grip. "What the fuck, man? What the *actual* fuck?"

His body shook as I grappled with him, both of us more or less matched in strength. I kept talking to him, willing him to snap out of whatever it was he was going through. "Kian. Talk to me."

Abruptly his struggles stopped. "If I do this, they might come home."

Fuck.

Those eight words, spoken with so much despair, told me everything I needed to know for now.

I squeezed his shoulders, before releasing him. The alarm still blared around us as I left Kian slumped against the car and strode to the side of the garage, where a thick, heavy chain lock hung on the wall above a motorcycle. Lifting it from its hook, I tested the weight in my palm, running my thumb across the attached padlock, before a slow smile spread across my face. I crossed the garage back to Kian at a run, jumping up onto the hood of the car and swinging the chain with all my might, smashing it down on top of the roof.

My whole focus narrowed to the swing of the chain, and the thunk as it hit the car roof over and over, marring and denting the metal, until I became aware of Kian, up on the hood of the car with me. He reached out, gripping my arms and stopping my movements. "We need to leave. Someone will have called the police by now."

I allowed him to take the chain from my hands and tug me down to the floor, the adrenaline leaving my body in a sudden rush. On autopilot, I stepped towards the garage door, but he pulled me in the opposite direction, to an interior door with a panel next to it.

As we came to a stop in front of the door and Kian placed his right hand on the fingerprint sensor, I realised his other hand was holding mine.

The door clicked open and he dropped my hand, pushing me into what looked like a utility room. I turned back in time to see him face the blinking security camera in the garage. He pushed his mask up on top of his head and flipped off the camera, then spun around and slammed the door to the garage shut behind him.

"We'll go out the back." He took a step towards me. Then another. Reaching out, he pushed up my mask, his eyes seeking out mine. The corners of his lips lifted into a crooked grin, and I felt my own answering smile tugging at my lips. "How did it feel? Breaking the rules?"

"With you?" My smile widened. "I think I like it."

He leaned his head forwards, just the tiniest bit, but it was enough to make his nose brush against my own. His breath hit my lips as his words came out in a husky rasp.

"I think I like corrupting you, Golden Boy."

SIX

PRESTON

"We never uploaded our prank." Kian threw the words out casually as we made our way down the winding cliff pathway that led down to the cove.

"Wait." Stopping dead, I gripped his bicep. "The whole Halloween pranks contest was your idea, wasn't it?"

He scuffed the dirt path with his toe. "Yeah—mine and Carter's. But it's not important. Not anymore." His raven hair, ruffled by the sea breeze, fell across his forehead as he turned and smirked at me. "I might've taken one or two photos of you going all Rambo on my dad's Bentley. Maybe I'll upload one as my entry."

I gave him a warning look. "Don't even think about it." Shoving his shoulder playfully as I moved past him to continue down the path, I added, "If anything, it'd be my entry since I'm the one in the photo."

He didn't reply because by now we'd reached the bottom of the cliff and he was being carried away from me into the crowds of people. Someone thrust a beer into my hand, and I popped the top, lifting it to my mouth.

As I drank, I stared around me curiously. We were in a

small, sandy cove, accessed by a tiny cliff path. Over to my left I could see the outline of what appeared to be a large cave entrance in the rocky cliff face, and beyond that there was a natural archway where the cliff had eroded, leading through to what I guessed might be another beach. People were grouped around a huge bonfire, music and talking mingling with the sound of the waves lapping at the shore. Colourful glowsticks littered the beach and decorated people's bodies, most (other than the guys who had been a part of our Fright Night plans) clad in costumes, in true Halloween style.

"Want some company?" Anastasia Egerton, one of the hottest and most popular girls in Alstone High, stood in front of me, dressed in some kind of leather catsuit, glowsticks looped around her blonde head like a halo. Giving me a suggestive smile, she pressed her body against mine, sliding her hand up my chest.

Oh, man. "Sorry." I placed my hand over hers and lifted it away from my body. "I'm, uh, gay."

Her mouth fell into an O. "I had no idea."

"Yeah, well..." I shrugged. "I haven't broadcast it. Being the new guy and all."

She nodded. "You don't have to explain. I won't say anything, despite what you might think of me. I wouldn't share something like that."

I took in her earnest gaze. I was well aware of her reputation for being bitchy and spreading rumours, but I trusted my instincts, and I was sure she was telling the truth right now.

"I think...I think I'm ready for people to know." It was time for me to be brave. My reasons I'd had for keeping it a secret suddenly didn't seem so important.

"In that case..." A devious smile spread across her face. "Come and meet the boys."

What boys?

She led me over to a small group of guys and girls, all in costume, sitting on blankets on the sand, and pointed everyone out to me. "Tom, Louis, Bilal, Emma, Claire. Everyone, this is Preston Montgomery III." I didn't recognise any of them, and I was just about to ask her if they attended Alstone High, when she turned back to me. "We all know each other from our polo club."

"Water polo?"

"No." She rolled her eyes and laughed. "Polo. With horses. You know?"

Ah, *that* polo. "Yeah, I know."

"Anyway, Tom and Louis are both single, studying for degrees in architecture so, you know...you get brains as well as beauty." They both eyed me curiously as I stood next to her. "And I happen to know that Louis is *very* good with his tongue," she purred.

"Oh, bloody hell, Ana. Please stop." The guy dressed as Thor—going by the red cape and the hammer lying in the sand next to him—pulled a face, his cheeks flushing slightly as he looked up at me. "Ignore her, I beg you."

I collapsed onto the blanket next to him as the others fell back into conversation, and he stared down at his beer bottle, picking at the label. "Louis. Good to meet you, Preston. I take it from your accent that you're not from around here?"

"Good to meet you, too. And nope." After placing my own bottle on the sand, I stretched my legs out in front of me and leaned back on my elbows. "US born and bred. Moved over here during the summer."

His eyes raked over me appreciatively, and I took the

chance to study him. Soft, wavy chestnut hair, warm brown eyes, and a long, lithe body; he might have been my type, once upon a time. Before tonight had happened.

Before Kian.

"How are you finding the UK so far? If you're free this weekend, I could take you to see some of the sights? There's a ruined castle up on the cliffs that could be fun to explore. Plenty of hidden nooks to get up close and personal."

My attention was temporarily diverted by someone's gaze boring holes into the side of my skull. Turning my head, my eyes met a pair of pale green ones that were darkening with anger as he stared at me sitting with Louis.

Raising a challenging brow, I cocked my head at him. He glared at me before dropping his gaze to the sand.

I suppressed the disappointment rising in me as I returned my attention to Louis. "I'm not interested in dating anyone right now. But if you wanna hang out as friends, I'm all for it."

"If friends is all you're offering, I'll take it. Shame, though," he murmured. His voice dropped and he leaned closer to me. "I could've shown you my legendary tongue skills."

There was silence for a beat, and then we both started laughing at the same time.

"Preston."

I stopped mid-laugh, bolting upright to see Kian towering over me. His face was a carefully blank mask, but his eyes...I could see the turmoil in them.

"What do you want, Kian?" I played it casual.

"Can I speak to you?"

"Sounds like you already are." Staring up at him, I couldn't help taunting him with my words.

"Fucking forget it," he muttered. Turning on his heel, he stalked away in the direction of the cliff face.

"Awkward." Louis fake-coughed from next to me.

For fuck's sake. "I'd better go after him." Climbing to my feet, I addressed the group. "Great meeting you guys. Catch you later." They gave me friendly nods and waves, and I smiled before heading towards the cliffs.

Up ahead, I saw Kian slip through the rock arch and disappear from sight. I increased my pace, not wanting to lose him out here on this darkened stretch of beach.

"Kian," I called out as I ducked through the archway and onto the small sliver of beach on the other side. "Kian?"

A dark shadow materialised from the rock face, and then I was pushed back against the cliff, and Kian's lips descended on mine, hard and hungry.

SEVEN

KIAN

Preston froze in shock for a second but recovered almost instantly. His smoothly shaven skin grazed against my own rough stubble as our mouths collided, his lips confidently stroking over mine, firm and sure.

From the first taste, I wanted more.

I attacked him with aggressive need, my lust for him out of control now I'd stopped fighting against it. My cock was like steel against his rigid length as we ground our bodies against one another.

"Fuck." I tore my mouth away, my heart pounding. "*Preston.*"

"You want to stop?" He stared at me, doubt entering his hypnotic blue eyes.

"Fuck, no."

"Good. Because I want to do this." He gripped my jaw and brought my face to his. Sparks of heat shot straight to my dick as he dragged his tongue over my lip piercing, then took my bottom lip between his teeth.

"I've been wondering how that lip ring would feel against my cock."

The low timbre of his voice sent a shudder of lust through me, and I stifled a groan. Everything he was saying and doing was driving me completely fucking *insane*.

"I want you." I pressed my body into his, my mouth on his neck, sucking hard enough to break the skin and leave my mark there. It wasn't enough. My hands fumbled at the buckle of his belt as I released my mouth from his neck, panting against him as his hand slid under my clothes, raking his fingers over the ridges of my abs.

"Kian...fuck." His tortured moan as I undid his jeans gave me confidence.

"I don't know what I'm doing, but I'm gonna try my hardest to make you feel so fucking good." I pushed his jeans down and gripped his cock through his boxers.

He hissed, sinking his teeth into my neck, his control slipping as I gave his cock an experimental stroke. It was kind of weird touching a dick from this angle, but I went with what I knew I liked, figuring he'd tell me if I did anything wrong. Easing down his boxers, I took his cock in my hand again. His hands went to my jeans, but I shook my head. "I want to concentrate. If you touch me, I'm gonna blow my load."

He groaned, his head falling back against the rock behind him, and I latched onto his neck again, sucking and licking over his skin as I stroked him up and down, slow and sure. "I've never touched another guy's dick before."

A low rumble of laughter escaped him, before he groaned again. "Don't stop. Damn, Kian. You drive me crazy."

"The feeling's mutual." Bringing someone else pleasure never felt so good. He thrust up into my hand, and I increased the pace a little. I felt him stiffen, and then he came with a roar, hot jets of cum covering my hand and soaking my hoodie.

"Shit, sorry." Breathing heavily, he stared down between us.

"No big deal." I shrugged, stepping back from him and tugging my hoodie off. "Use it to clean up if you want."

"You're so sexy." His eyes trailed down my body, and my cock pounded against my jeans. "Can I touch you?"

"You're asking for my permission now, after you not only pinned me up against the wall, *twice*, but came all over my hand?" I raised a brow, and he gave me a lopsided grin as he buttoned up his jeans.

"Yeah. Better late than never, huh?"

Swallowing hard, I stared him straight in the eyes, deadly serious. "I really, really fucking want you to touch me. Show me your skills, Golden Boy."

His grin faded. He took the hoodie from my hands, tossing it to the ground. "Get ready to have your mind blown."

"I'm hearing a lot of talk, but not seeing any action," I taunted him, and his eyes darkened as he moved closer. He licked across the metal of my lip ring again, pulling me to him.

"I can feel how much you want me." He thrust his hips against mine, both of us breathing hard as he ran his hands down my chest and over my abs, stopping at the top of my jeans. His fingers made quick work of undoing them, and finally, he freed my aching cock, and wrapped his hand around me.

At his first touch, I groaned, bucking into his hand. "Harder."

"How about this instead?" He claimed my mouth with a savage kiss.

Then, tearing his mouth away from mine, he dropped to his knees in the sand.

He looked up at me for a moment with a heavy, lustful gaze, before wrapping his lips around my cock. My fingers gripped his short hair as he plunged forwards, taking my entire length into his throat.

"Oh, *fuck*." My balls tightened and I came down his throat, my dick jerking in his mouth as he swallowed everything I gave him.

He released my cock and straightened up, wiping his mouth as I collapsed back against the rock face on shaking legs. Once I got my breath back, I pulled him to me. "I've never...fuck, Preston. I've never come so fast in my life. I couldn't hold out. As soon as you had your mouth on me, it was game over."

A slow, satisfied smile spread across his face, and he pressed a kiss to my jaw. "I'll take it as a compliment. I got you wound up so tightly that you were ready to explode."

"Yeah, maybe. Kind of embarrassing, though," I muttered.

"Hey, I didn't last much longer." His mouth moved to my neck, and he licked across my skin, making me shiver. "That was the best damn hand job I've ever had."

"Yeah?"

He raised his head to look at me. "Yeah. I said it before, and I'll say it again. You drive me crazy, Kian Courtland." Reaching out his hand, he took mine, and pressed it to the bulge straining against his jeans. "See what you do to me?"

My own cock stirred as I lightly squeezed him through his jeans, extracting a low moan from his mouth. I leaned closer to him. "I don't know what the fuck I'm doing, but I don't want to stop."

"Want to come home with me? We'll have the house to

ourselves all night." He spoke the words against my lips, his voice a suggestive rumble that had me zipping up my jeans at a record rate and flying over to where my hoodie lay discarded on the sand. I picked it up, shaking the sand off it, and tucked it under my arm. Turning back to Preston, I met his hungry gaze.

We stared at one another for a long, charged moment.

"Let's go."

EIGHT

PRESTON

Kian had been silent on the drive back to my house, but when we were standing by my front door, he finally spoke. "I take it you like Halloween?"

My gaze swept over the front yard—the path lined with pumpkins, the wreath of browns and oranges hanging on the door, and the matching garlands draped across the porch and down the columns on either side.

"Yeah. This is nothing compared to the decorations we had back home, but we wanted to do something. My mom lives for this stuff; she decorates for all the seasons." I indicated to the door. "This is her fall wreath. As soon as December comes, she'll switch it out for the winter wreath. She's obsessed." Turning my head, I saw him watching me with an odd expression. "What?"

He shook his head, huffing out a laugh. "Nothing. Just the way you call autumn 'fall' in your sexy accent...it's really fucking hot."

I stared at him. "Says the guy with the hot British accent. There's nothing special about the way I speak."

"Let's agree to disagree," he said, narrowing his eyes at

me, and I laughed as I turned away from him to unlock the door.

"Sure. Come on in. You want a drink or anything?" Stepping through the door and into the hallway, I dropped my keys into the bowl and pulled off my hoodie. "Kian?"

Strong arms came around me from behind, and Kian's breath fell across my earlobe. "Why don't we skip the polite talk and you show me your bedroom?"

Damn, when he spoke to me that way...I'd do anything he asked.

"Okay."

Closing my bedroom door behind us, I turned to him. He stood against the wall, worrying at his lip ring.

"We don't have to do anything you don't want."

He pulled me to him, his arms going around my waist. "I want it. I'm just...I need a minute. It's a lot to process."

Leaning forwards, I ran my nose across his jaw, feeling the scratch of stubble on my skin. "We can take things as slow as you want." The whole night so far had left my head spinning, so I wasn't surprised he was having trouble getting his head around everything. "My parents won't be back until tomorrow afternoon. Take as much time as you need. You're the one in control here."

"Yeah?" he rasped, trailing hot kisses down my neck. "What if I want you to control me?"

I ground my hips against his. "You like that, huh?"

"I don't know. But I like *you*." His voice shook slightly, and my stomach flipped at his words. We were on the same page. It wasn't only sexual chemistry between us. There was something more.

I waited until he lifted his head, and then I ran my tongue over his lip ring again, before kissing him. "You know I like you, right?"

Our eyes met, and he nodded slowly. "The way you haven't been able to take your eyes off me since the first day we met was kind of a giveaway." He smirked, and I leaned into him, tugging his earlobe between my teeth.

"What can I say? You're easy on the eyes. You've got that hot bad-boy vibe going for you."

"I am, and I do."

"Arrogant, too."

"Sometimes."

We were both grinning by now, and the apprehension had disappeared from his eyes. After dropping a light kiss on his lips, I made a suggestion. "You want a shower? Start off slow."

He frowned.

"A shower with me," I clarified.

"Oh. Showering together is starting off slow, is it?" He nipped at my bottom lip.

"I've got a wet room."

"Lead the way."

Laughing at the enthusiasm in his voice, I pointed him towards my bathroom. "You go ahead and get the shower running. I'll get some fresh towels."

I took my time getting the towels and undressing, figuring I'd give him some space. I wasn't sure how this was all going to play out, but I'd take my cues from him and go with it. We'd need to discuss things at some point, but not yet. Right now, I had a hot as fuck guy naked and wet in my shower, and he was waiting for me.

The glass separating the shower area from the rest of the bathroom was steamy, obscuring my vision, but what I could make out made my cock stir. As I rounded the side of the glass, I sucked in a harsh breath, my cock rising to full mast as I took in the most erotic sight I'd ever seen in my life.

Kian Courtland, all lean, hard, male perfection, head bowed under the shower spray, one hand planted on the wall, and the other fisting his erect cock.

He turned his head as I entered. Water plastered his dark hair to his head, running down his face. I followed the rivulets of water streaking down his body, over the sculpted muscles, through the light trail of hair leading down to his erection. My mouth was suddenly dry, and I ached for him.

"Fuuuuck, Golden Boy." He licked his lips, his heated gaze raking over me. "Your body is *insane*."

"Kian." My groan echoed through the wet room. I crossed to him. "You're—" I was speechless for the first time in my life. "You're incredible," I said eventually, reaching down between us and aligning my hardness with his. I wrapped my hand around both of our cocks, and he flexed his fingers under mine, stretching his hand to encompass my cock as well as his, following my direction.

"This feels amazing." He stared down between us, his eyes heavy-lidded, his pupils blown, tracking our combined movements. The friction of his dick sliding against mine, and his hand on me, was the best kind of torture. If Kian's rasping breaths were anything to go by, he was feeling the same.

"Yeah? You like that, huh?"

"Too much. I don't know if I'm gonna last." He looked up to meet my gaze, before inclining his head to kiss me. "You're killing me here."

A smile spread across my face. Releasing my grip, I

stopped his movements with my hand. "Let's slow it down. Turn around."

"Turn around?" His voice was suddenly alarmed, and I smirked at him. Picking up the bottle of shower gel from the shelf, I waved it in the air. Relief broke across his face. "I thought..."

"I know what you thought. Don't worry, I'm not going to fuck you. I'm not going to do anything you don't want." Gripping his shoulders, I turned him, directing him under the spray, and picked up a washcloth. I ran it over his back in slow, circular movements, taking my time.

"I'm not saying I wouldn't want you to." His low murmur was barely discernible over the sound of running water. "I might. I mean, I think I do. I need to work up to it, though."

I stopped what I was doing and slid my arms around him. "Whatever you want." My voice lowered as I pressed against him, my hard cock against his ass. "Your ass is spectacular. But I don't have any expectations here. You're in control, remember."

He pushed his ass back into me, and I growled, nipping at his shoulder. "But right now, you're really fucking tempting me." I heard a low chuckle come out of him, the bastard. "You like being a cocktease, do ya?"

"Seems so. Me and my spectacular ass."

The corners of my mouth tugged up into a smile. "You're different. Different to how I thought."

He turned in my arms, facing me with his dark brows pulled together. "What's that supposed to mean?"

"In a good way. You're not the angry bad boy that looked like he wanted to stab me in my sleep."

His face cleared, and he eyed me with a devious grin. "I think you like it when I'm bad." Twisting his arms around me, he ran his fingers up the back of my neck and through my wet hair. "I like it when *you're* bad. When you go up against me and don't back down." He kissed me, hard. "When you get me all riled up."

"You like that?"

"Mmm, yeah. All that sexual tension." He flexed his hips, and we both groaned.

"Kian..."

"Turn around, Golden Boy, and let me wash you."

I complied, and as he worked his large hands over my shoulders with firm, sure strokes, I closed my eyes. How was this happening? This...thing...between us—it felt so *right*. All I could do was hope that he felt the same way.

Every single thought flew out of my mind when he pressed the full length of his body against my back, grinding his cock against my ass. He pulled me back against him, his arms coming around me. Running his hands down over my chest and abs, he stopped, right above my cock.

I heard him exhale harshly, before he brought his mouth to my ear.

"I want to fuck you."

Turning my head, I captured his mouth in a hard, lustful kiss, before I reluctantly pulled away. "You don't know how much I want that." I swallowed thickly. "But I think we should take it slow."

Disappointment flared in his gaze, but then he nodded reluctantly. "You're right. But, fuck, Preston. I just...*fuck*." He ground his cock against my ass again. "I want this. You. Everything."

"You can have me. I just don't want you to regret anything."

"The only thing I regret is the way I acted around you

before tonight." He bent his head to my throat, kissing, sucking and licking his way up to my jaw.

"Let's forget about that," I managed to pant out, as he nipped at my jaw, running his hand over the muscles of my pecs and circling my nipples.

"It's forgotten." His breathing grew harsher, and his voice was a low rasp when his next words came out. "If you're not going to let me fuck you, can I suck your cock?"

NINE

KIAN

I followed Preston into his bedroom, unable to take my eyes off his firm ass, the muscles flexing as he walked. Fuck me, he was hot. When I'd been pressed against him in the shower, feeling his hard, strong body against mine, all I could think was that I wanted my dick inside him.

I still wanted it. He was probably right to make me wait, but his intentions were misguided. If he thought I'd regret anything we'd done or were going to do, he was completely fucking wrong.

He stopped at the edge of his bed, turning to me, and I took a minute to admire him. Blond hair, still damp from the shower, and water still glistening on his skin. His muscles were sharply defined, carved from hours of football and dedicated gym time. Yeah, I could admit now that I'd checked him out while we were training. And his cock...my mouth watered as I drank in the sight of his long, thick erection, precum beading at the tip.

"Are you just going to stand there, or are you gonna suck my dick?" One eyebrow pulled up, and I shook my head.

"Someone's impatient."

"Kian."

The way he growled my name, like he was barely restraining himself, sent a shudder of lust down my spine. I prowled towards him, watching his sapphire eyes darken to black, his Adam's apple bobbing as he swallowed.

Stopping right in front of him, I traced my hand down his chest, feeling his heart racing under my palm. "At the beach, you said you were wondering how my lip ring would feel against your cock."

He groaned low in his throat.

"Lie back and you'll find out."

I'd never seen him move so fast. One minute he was in front of me, the next he was on the bed, head propped on the pillows, staring at me with hungry eyes.

My hard-on was really fucking painful at this point, but I ignored it for now. If I got my way, I'd be fucking him sooner rather than later. Kneeling on the bed, I took his cock in my hand, hearing a strangled curse slip past his lips. I lowered my head, taking my time to prolong the torture, and his hand fisted the sheet next to him. Once again, I didn't have any experience, but I had confidence in the way he reacted to everything I was doing to him.

I took a slow, experimental lick across the tip, tasting his salty flavour for the first time. "Oh, fuck," he groaned, his hips jerking up. Drawing back, I looked up at him staring down at me, and I smiled.

"Do you have any lube?"

His eyes widened, and his teeth dug into his bottom lip. He nodded, and I gave one, slow, glide of my hand along his cock, then released it. "Give it to me."

Rolling to the side, he fumbled in his bedside drawer, handing me a plastic bottle with a pump dispenser. I coated my fingers, noting the way he was watching every movement like a hawk, his chest rising and falling with unsteady breaths.

I lowered my head again, and this time I dragged my lip over the head of his cock, the smooth metal of my piercing sliding across his sensitive tip.

"*Kian*." His tortured plea went straight to my dick, and I shifted position, lowering my head to encompass more of him in my mouth while my hand went to my own erection. I tentatively flattened my tongue on the underside of his shaft, and he bucked his hips again, sending his cock to the back of my mouth. Drawing back, I suppressed the urge to cough and then went in again, taking more of him into my mouth, using his reactions to guide me. I gripped my dick, stroking up and down, and Preston moaned again. "This is the hottest thing I've ever seen. Your mouth around my cock while you touch yourself." His legs stiffened. "Fuck, I don't think I can—"

I released him, sitting up, and he stared down at me, his eyes wild. "What are you doing?"

"Experimenting." I smirked, and he glared at me. Yeah, he didn't like that very much. I leaned over him to lightly bite his jaw, and then he suddenly flipped us both so he was lying on top of me, our bodies pressed together.

"You're infuriatingly sexy," he rasped in my ear, rocking against me. Shifting lower down my body, he kissed his way down my neck and onto my chest, where he tugged my nipple between his teeth, making me hiss. He released it, kissing lower and lower, his tongue dragging over the ridges of my abs. "I'm obsessed with this, right here." His fingers went to the small trail of dark hair that led to my cock, and he stroked downwards, wrapping his hand around my hard length. *Fuck.*

He slowly pumped his hand up and down, then took me into his mouth and lightly gripped my balls.

"Fucking hell, Golden Boy." Now I was the one bucking my hips into his mouth, and a gleam of satisfaction entered his eyes as he worked his mouth over me. With an effort, I took a handful of his hair between my fingers and tugged.

He released me, raising a brow. "Problem?"

"Lie back. I want to try something." I added another generous pump of lube to my fingertips, and when he was lying flat on his back, I crawled between his spread legs. "How would you feel about me doing this?" Sliding my finger into his crease, I pressed it against his hole.

His mouth fell open, and I took that as assent, pushing my finger inside in tiny, slow increments. Fuck, he was tight. I had zero experience with this, but I did know that if I wanted my cock to fit inside him, he needed to be ready.

A string of curse words fell from his lips as I eased my finger inside him, and I lowered my head to his cock, taking him into my mouth again. His hands came down to grip my hair, and he stroked his fingers over my scalp.

"You're incredible." He swallowed thickly. "Your finger feels so good. And your mouth. I want more."

Slowly, carefully, I eased another finger inside, waiting for him to relax again before I started to move them. I lifted my head from his cock. "Is this okay? Am I hurting you?"

"It stings a bit, but it feels so fucking good," he panted, his grip on my hair tightening. I worked my fingers inside him, stretching him out. His low moans and pants filled the room, and I couldn't take it anymore.

"I need my cock inside you. Now."

His eyes met mine, his expression tortured. "You don't

know how much I want you in me, but I don't want to rush this."

"I want it. I want you." I withdrew my fingers almost all the way, then thrust them in again. The lube and the work I'd done stretching him out helped my fingers to slide in easily this time, and he gasped as I pushed them all the way in.

"*Yes*. Right there." His eyes rolled back. "Fuck me, please."

Finally.

Prepared with a condom and lube, I took a moment to appreciate the sight of Preston sprawled against the sheets, hot and ready for me. Leaning over him, I ran my hands over his thighs, his muscles tense under my palms. "Ready?" He nodded. "Get on your knees, Golden Boy."

I positioned myself behind him, running my hands over his spread ass. His powerful back arched, muscles flexing as he supported himself on his hands and knees. "I'm gonna make us both feel so fucking good," I promised, aligning the head of my cock with his hole.

"Go slow." His voice was a hoarse whisper.

I pushed forwards, meeting the resistance of his body, but he rocked backwards, taking the tip inside.

We both groaned. "Fuck, Preston. This already feels fucking incredible." I reached around to stroke his cock, holding myself in place. My dick was throbbing, desperate to be all the way inside him, but I held off.

"More," he hissed. "Give me more."

I flexed my hips, pushing further in, and he rocked back again, until I was finally buried inside his hot, tight hole.

Nothing had ever felt so good. *Nothing*. "Fuck," I muttered, looking down at the view of my cock inside him. Withdrawing almost all the way out, I paused for a second, then thrust all the way in.

"Kian, *fuuuuck*." Preston's voice was raw and so fucking hot, that I moaned. "Right there. Harder."

That was when I really started to move, my hips thrusting forwards, in and out, as he pushed back against me. I reached around to grip his cock again, my hand stroking harder and faster as I fucked him.

"I don't ever want to stop," I whispered harshly. "You feel so good."

He looked over his shoulder and our eyes met. "Don't stop."

Releasing his dick, I pistoned my hips even harder. He pressed his upper body down into the mattress, his groans muffled by the pillow as I braced myself with my arms either side of him.

Reaching down, he began pumping his cock as I fucked him, and I was done for.

"*Fuck*, Preston." My balls tightened, and my release spilled inside him, sending him over the edge. He clenched around me, hot cum shooting from his dick onto the sheets as he called out my name.

Panting, I eased out of him, and let him roll over onto his back before lowering myself onto his body. Our mingled breaths came fast and ragged, and sweat dripped from my hair onto his face.

I paused, attempting to calm my racing heart, and our eyes met.

He reached up and brushed my hair out of my eyes, then tugged me down to him so our foreheads pressed together. His low rumble vibrated against my chest.

"I don't ever want to stop, either."

A smile spread across my face, and I pressed a kiss to his lips, feeling his answering smile as his arms tightened around me.

I raised my head so I could meet his eyes.

"You're fucking *mine* now, Golden Boy."

TEN

PRESTON

Stretching, I rolled to the right, bleary-eyed, to check my phone. 7:06 a.m. Way, way too early. I groaned under my breath, rolling back towards the centre of the bed.

A pair of pale green eyes blinked sleepily at me.

"What time is it?" His voice was raspy from lack of sleep, and I smiled.

"Too early. Go back to sleep."

His eyelids fluttered shut, and I sighed in relief. I wanted to stay in this bubble forever.

My gaze trailed over his tousled hair, down his face, and onto his exposed chest.

"You're staring."

"Sorry."

His eyes blinked open again, and he yawned. "I feel like I've only had two hours' sleep."

"That's probably because you have." After everything that had gone down between us last night, we'd showered and I'd changed the sheets, and then we lay awake for hours, talking until one or both of us had finally succumbed to sleep around five in the morning.

We looked at one another silently for a moment, then the questions that had been rolling around in my head came out in a rush. "What happens next? What is this thing between us?"

He rubbed at his face, then rolled onto his side, propping himself up on his elbow. "First off, I like you. I want to see where this thing goes." His hand traced a pattern over my chest. "I've never been with a guy before, but I...I've been interested. Everything that we've done—it feels right. Like it was meant to be. I never had that with a girl before."

I reached up and pushed his hair out of his eyes as he continued speaking, his voice going quiet. "I don't even think it's because you're a guy. I think it's because it's *you*."

Swallowing hard around the lump in my throat, I stared at him. "I want this. What about school?"

His gaze turned serious. "Fuck, I don't know. Can we take it slow, see what happens? I don't want to hide, but I want...time, I guess."

"Time. I can give you that."

"You sure you want to be with a delinquent? I might be a bad influence on you." He smirked, and I pulled him down to me.

"You sure you want to be with an American who can kick your ass on the soccer field?"

"You calling football 'soccer' might be a deal breaker." I growled at that, biting at his bottom lip, and he laughed in response. "Wait 'til I'm back from my suspension. You and me, we're gonna be unstoppable. The dream team."

"Only if you don't try and hog the limelight."

"Never."

"Have you looked in the mirror today?" Kian asked me around a mouthful of toast.

"No, why?" I stared at him over my mug of coffee.

He finished chewing, then grinned at me. "You might wanna check out your neck."

I picked up my phone and turned on the selfie camera. "What the fuck, man?" My neck was covered in purple hickeys. "I can't leave the house looking like this."

"Wear a scarf," he suggested with a laugh, picking up his coffee and taking a large gulp, before placing it back on the kitchen island. The bastard was enjoying this. "I like my marks on you."

"Yeah? What if I leave one on you?"

"Go ahead." He shrugged, tilting his head to the side, his eyes sparking with amusement.

I slid off my bar stool and crossed the island to him. My arm snaked around his waist, and I put my mouth to his neck, licking across his skin.

"Come here." His voice lowered, and he tugged me between his legs. Breakfast forgotten, he gripped my jaw and kissed me.

Hot, heady kisses, his tongue against mine, his hands gripping me tightly...I couldn't get enough of this guy. He broke the kiss, panting, and I went for his throat, sucking at the skin while he groaned, his hand going down between us to my sweatpants.

"So fucking hard already," he husked. "I want—" His phone suddenly blared loudly, vibrating against the wooden surface of the island.

"Shit. It's my dad."

I went to pull away from him, but he held me in place while he answered the call. I could only hear his side of it, but the voice on the other end sounded angry.

"Yeah?... Fine... Whatever, it's not like you care... You're not coming home?" His shoulders slumped, and my arms tightened around him. He listened intently to the voice, his jaw clenched, his eyes darkening.

Then he was speaking, low and furious. "You didn't appreciate seeing me holding hands with a man? Guess fucking what?" He took a harsh breath, then snarled the words that left me reeling. "That's my boyfriend, *so get fucking used to it.*" With that, he ended the call, throwing his phone down on the island. His head dropped to my shoulder, and I held on to him tightly until his breathing slowed and his arms loosened.

He drew back to look at me. "Sorry you had to hear that." His voice was raw and defeated. "My dad...he's a fucking asshole. Both my parents are. I don't know why I keep trying. They couldn't even be bothered to show up for my eighteenth birthday."

"What?" I couldn't keep the shock from my tone.

"Yeah. They said we'd go out, make the most of my status as a legal adult at some amazing Michelin-starred restaurant, but neither of them bothered to show." His voice cracked, and it fucking broke me.

"You have me, now." I inclined my head to kiss him. "You know, I only got to celebrate my eighteenth with my parents. It wasn't long after we'd moved here, and I didn't know anyone yet. What do you say we plan an epic party? Celebrate both our birthdays, or whatever other excuse you want. Make up for it?"

"Yeah." He nodded. "Yeah. Fuck, yeah. Let's do it." His lips slammed onto mine.

When he pulled away, he was smiling. "Thanks for making me feel better."

I returned his smile. "Anytime." My eyes searched his,

and I took a deep breath. "Did you mean what you said to your dad on the phone, by the way, or was that just to rile him up?"

One eyebrow pulled up. He gave me a knowing grin. "Oh, yeah. I meant it, *boyfriend*. We might be taking things slow, but I only want you."

"And I sure as hell don't want anyone else."

"That's settled, then." His smile turned satisfied. "I think we need to celebrate our new relationship status."

"Yeah? What did you have in mind?" My words faded to a hoarse whisper, as his mouth went to my throat.

Drawing back, he licked his lips, slowly, deliberately, as his heated gaze ran over my body.

He reached down to the waistband of my sweatpants.

"I have a few ideas..."

ELEVEN

KIAN

NOVEMBER

"Morning." Preston's fingers brushed mine as he passed me on the front steps of Alstone High, where I was standing with Carter and Xavier.

"Morning." This was going to be harder than I thought. I hadn't seen him since I'd left his place on Saturday, before his parents came home. He seemed to understand my need for space, to process everything that had happened. Before Halloween I was Kian Courtland, Alstone High's resident fuck-up and disappointment to my parents. Now, I was still me, but Preston had managed to work his way under my skin, and I'd somehow ended up with a boyfriend. I'd been raging at my dad when I'd told him Preston was my boyfriend, and the words had just come out without any conscious thought, but as soon as I said them, I meant them. What was the point in denying it? I wanted him, he wanted me and there was no reason to pretend otherwise. I knew he had his doubts about whether I wanted to get into a relationship so quickly, but the truth was, from the second I'd kissed him, I knew he was different. Before that, even, if I was being honest with myself. No one had ever affected me the way he did, and the truth was, being with him felt so fucking right, that I couldn't even consider *not* being with him. Not after Friday night.

Staring after him, I watched him enter the building, and all I wanted was to go with him. Hold his hand, announce to the world that he was mine.

But I couldn't do it.

It was too fucking hard.

My attention was off all morning. I was on edge, my head pounding. Were people looking at me differently? Did they know? What would happen if I told everyone I was bi?

The second I sat down in the cafeteria at lunchtime, Preston's eyes met mine, and I could tell he knew I was on the verge of panic. I couldn't breathe—I needed to get away. Smoke, drink, smash something up...anything to stop my brain from overthinking, twisting me in these knots that wouldn't go away.

"Kian." His voice was soft but commanding, and the table went silent, looking between us. "Are we still training over lunch?"

Carter cut in, which was good because at that moment I seemed to have lost the ability to speak. "Since when are you two friends?"

Preston glanced at him, then back to me. His eyes were dark and worried, but a small smile briefly curved over his lips, and yeah, I wanted to kiss him right then. "I don't know if 'friends' is exactly the word I'd use...but we've come to a... uh...an understanding. Right, Kian?"

Pulling my lip ring between my teeth, I nodded mutely, and Carter raised a brow. "Miracles do happen, after all."

There was a ringing in my ears. Preston said something about me showing him some of my tricks on the pitch, but I couldn't concentrate on anything. I needed to get out of here, to catch my breath.

"Kian." Preston's voice cut through the white noise, and I stared at him. "Want to go now?"

My lunch was forgotten as I grabbed my bag and stood and began walking towards the doors. Behind me, I heard the scrape as Preston pushed his chair back, and someone calling me a "moody bugger," but I ignored all that. I needed to get out of there. Now.

Preston caught up with me as I was stalking across the quad. "Follow me." He led me through the school grounds towards the gym, but instead of heading inside, he took me around the back, where we were finally alone. Stopping, he dropped his bag to the floor and leaned against the wall, his hands in his pockets. The breeze ruffled his blond hair as he scuffed his toe against the floor. "Are you okay? Are you having second thoughts about us?"

My eyes flew to his, seeing the concern and apprehension written all over his face. He wouldn't look at me.

"Golden Boy." Dropping my own bag, I stopped in front of him. I took a deep breath, filling my lungs with much-needed air, before I cupped his chin in my hand, forcing him to look at me. Planting my other hand on the wall next to him, I ran my thumb across his jaw. "There's no fucking way I'm giving you up."

His whole body seemed to relax, and I stepped closer, sliding my hand around the back of his neck. I nipped at his bottom lip, and he groaned, removing his hands from his pockets and pulling my hips into his. "If you are, though, please just tell—"

"I'm not." Pressing my mouth to his, I flicked my tongue against his lips, and he finally opened up for me. The voices in my head fell silent at last, and all I saw was him. This was worth whatever shit was coming. *He* was worth it.

Our kisses turned aggressive, hungry, as I pressed his body up against the wall. His cock, already hardening, rubbed up against mine, and he groaned into my mouth.

"Fuck, Preston." I moved my lips to his jaw, biting and licking across his skin as he rolled his hips against me. "I want—"

Shouts sounded from the other side of the gym building, and we sprang apart, both breathing heavily.

"We need to be somewhere else for this." Preston ran a hand down his face.

"Yeah. Like in your bed."

His eyes darkened as he stared at me, and I couldn't help leaning forwards and claiming his mouth again in a kiss that was way too short.

"This is harder than I thought it would be." He leaned back against the wall with a heavy sigh.

"Yeah, it's very hard." Smirking, I reached down and palmed his cock through his trousers, unable to help myself.

"Tease," he growled. "I'm gonna pay you back for torturing me like this."

Retreating to a safe distance where I wouldn't be tempted to touch him again, I met his eyes, willing my dick to behave, reminding myself where we were. "Being serious. I'm not having second thoughts about you. I'm just...I'm struggling to get my head around everything, okay?"

"I know, and I'm not going to pressure you. I said I'd give you as much time as you needed, and I meant it. It's just...we hadn't spoken, and..." He trailed off with another sigh, his mouth twisting.

"You're my boyfriend. That's not changing, unless you change your mind about us."

"Not gonna happen." He shook his head, a smile finally appearing on his face, which I returned.

"Come on, Golden Boy. Let me show you some of my football skills. That was why you wanted to get me alone during lunch, wasn't it?"

"It was the only excuse I could think of." Picking up his bag, he gave me a grin that made my stomach flip. I let my eyes trail over his body, taking my time to enjoy the sight of him filling out his uniform in all the right places.

"Fuck, you're hot."

His lips curved in amusement, but he deliberately raked his gaze over me. "So are you."

"I know."

He shook his head at me. "Come on, before your head gets any bigger. I want to see your ball skills in action."

"I know you like me playing with your balls." I gave him a suggestive smile as he passed me, and he laughed.

"Couldn't resist, huh?"

"Nope." We headed back around the gym entrance and used our passes to enter. "Did anyone notice your neck?"

He rolled his eyes. "Did anyone notice the mass of hickeys my boyfriend left all over me? Why would you think they would? They're barely even visible." Pushing the door to the changing room open, he indicated for me to go through first. "If you'd turned up in the cafeteria about five minutes earlier, you would've heard everyone joking about it." There were a few other guys in the changing room, and he lowered his voice. "I changed the subject to the Fright Night pranks the guys had pulled, and..." He shrugged. "Most of them like to talk about themselves."

"Yeah." We finished changing in silence, aware of the presence of the others around us, then headed out onto the football pitch. The repetition of the drills focused my mind as we passed the ball back and forth, but I knew I'd have to face up to things sooner or later.

We couldn't hide forever.

TWELVE

PRESTON

My phone buzzed, and I discreetly opened it, shielding the screen with my palm so I could read the message without anyone else seeing. Across the cafeteria table, I felt Kian's hot gaze boring into me, and I shifted in my seat.

Delinquent: Guess what I'm thinking about?

A smile played across my lips as I replied.

Me: What?
Delinquent: You. Me. In your shower

My cock twitched, and I bit back a groan. *Oh, man*. The effect this guy had on me... Blowing out a heavy breath, I kept my face neutral as my fingers flew over my phone keyboard.

Me: Mmm. I like your mind

Delinquent: Is it wrong that I'm hard right now?

My smile grew wider, even as I struggled to control my own reaction to the thought of Kian, across the table, getting hard from the thought of us together.

Delinquent: You look sexy when you smile, Golden Boy

Warmth spread through me, and before I knew it, I'd sent him the question I'd been wanting to ask him for a while now. The few weeks we'd been together had been better than anything I could've hoped or imagined, despite the fact we'd been sneaking around, sharing stolen moments between classes. We'd spent as much time together as we could out of school, though, and now, I wanted more. I wanted to share everything with him.

And that included my family.

Me: Want to meet my parents?

Across the table from me his eyes widened, and I heard his harsh intake of breath.

"You okay, mate?" Xavier raised a brow at him.

"Fine," Kian said brusquely, returning his attention to his phone.

Taking a bite of my sandwich, I kept an eye on my own phone, waiting for the message notification to come through. When two alerts came through in quick succession, I placed my sandwich down and swiped open our message thread, taking care to hide it from the guys next to me.

Delinquent: That killed my boner
Delinquent: Seriously??? You want me to meet them?
Me: 100%

I watched him closely as he played with his lip ring, having some kind of internal debate with himself. His fingers hovered over his phone for a moment, before he straightened up.

Delinquent: OK
Me: Good

When he looked up and met my eyes, I mouthed *thanks* across the table. He gave me a tiny smile that was almost shy, before lowering his gaze back to his phone.

Making a snap decision, I put it all out there.

Me: I want to tell the soccer team about me. Being gay
Delinquent: You sure?

We'd spoken a bit about it, and he knew I'd been planning to tell them, but something about Kian's willingness to meet my parents...I couldn't help thinking it was a significant step for us. And that meant I needed to be honest with everyone about who I was, otherwise, how could I ever hope that Kian would choose to be open about us, one day?

Me: Sure. I need to do this
Delinquent: OK. Start with Carter. He'll appre-

ciate the heads up since he's the captain and if you can get him on board the others will be easier

Delinquent: I've got your back. If you want me to speak to him with you I will

Me: Thanks. I've got this but I like knowing you're there for me

Delinquent: Always

Slipping my phone into my pocket, I turned to Carter, keeping my voice low so I didn't attract unwanted attention. "Can I have a quick word? In private?"

He gave me a curious look, but he answered immediately. "Yeah, of course." We both stood, and Kian gave me a small, reassuring nod. I headed outside to a table at the far side of the quad, where we wouldn't be overheard. My legs suddenly felt like they were going to give way, and I threw myself into a seat before Carter noticed.

He remained standing. I blew out a heavy breath, forcibly tensing my leg to stop it from bouncing. "Can you sit down? You're making me nervous."

As he sat down, I concentrated on breathing, trying to gather my thoughts. My stomach rolled.

Carter interrupted my thoughts. "Mate, spit it out. You're making *me* nervous, now."

Right.

Here goes nothing. "Sorry, man. I need to tell you something. I wanted to give you a heads-up, since you're the soccer team captain." I held his gaze, resting my elbows on the table in front of me. "A couple of people know already, but before rumours start spreading, I wanted to tell you myself. I'm...I'm gay. I want to tell the rest of the team. Get it out there, you know?"

The silence stretched uncomfortably. My mind flashed to my ex back in the US, and how the football team had taken the news that he was gay.

Fuck.

Before my thoughts spiralled into panic, Carter finally broke the silence, his eyes on mine, full of sincerity. "I've got your back. You want me to tell the team?"

My relief was instant. "I'll tell them. Do you... Do you think anyone will have a problem?"

His expression hardened. "If they have a problem, they'll have to fucking go through me. If anyone gives you a hard time, *anyone*, you come straight to me, okay? And if you want me to be there when you tell them, I will."

"Thanks, man. My ex...he, uh. His teammates didn't take it well when he came out to them. I'd appreciate it if you were there when I tell the others." I gave him a small smile.

"Consider it done. Most of the boys are sound, but I won't lie and say it'll be an easy ride. I'll be around to deal with anyone who gives you problems, though. We're a team." He rose to his feet and headed around the table to me. Placing a hand on my shoulder, he added, "Whenever you want to tell them, I'll be there."

I nodded my thanks, and we headed back inside. "Thanks for being cool with it," I murmured, then cast around for a change of subject. "Speaking of thanks, I never said thanks for organising the party."

My idea to belatedly celebrate Kian's and my birthdays was going ahead, and we'd roped in Ben, another guy on the soccer team, since his birthday was coming up. Kian and Carter had taken on the organisation, and I was happy to let them sort it all out. I didn't care what we did—all I cared about was putting a smile on Kian's face, and to show him that despite his parents' neglect, there were people that cared about him and wanted to celebrate with him.

"You're welcome." Carter gave me a quick grin as we reached our table. The sound of the bell to indicate the end of lunch hour swallowed up anything else I was going to say, and there was a flurry of activity as everyone grabbed their bags and headed to their respective classes.

"How did it go?" Kian asked me in a low voice as we made our way out of the cafeteria.

"Good. Better than I hoped."

"Good." He curled the tip of his finger over mine, his touch so brief that it was almost like I'd imagined it, before he was gone, swallowed by the crowd of students.

THIRTEEN

PRESTON

Lying on my bed, I scrolled through my phone, willing the time to go more quickly. Pausing on the message from my teammate Ben, I read through his words again, before tapping out a response.

Ben: Appreciate ur bravery today bro. It sucks that it should even be an issue but u never know how much speaking out will help someone else. Wish my cousin had someone like u around when he was at school
Me: I wish he had too. No one should have to struggle on their own. I appreciate your support. It means a lot

He sent me a thumbs-up emoji in reply, and I smiled, thinking back to earlier.

"Ready?" Carter spoke in a low voice, and I nodded. Standing in the locker room in front of the soccer team, with

all eyes on me after Carter's call for everyone's attention, the nerves returned in full force.

"You've got this." Kian's voice was barely a whisper, only for my ears, and it bolstered me. Flanked by two of the three kings of Alstone High, I cleared my throat, then spoke up.

"Hi. I, uh. We're a team, and I want...I want to be open and honest with you guys." My voice cracked, and I cleared my throat again. "I'm—I'm gay. Always have been. I just wanted to get it out there, in the interests of transparency."

Carter cut in as I finished stumbling over my words. "I want to make it clear that any kind of backlash, or homophobic slurs, or any behaviour that gives Preston cause for concern will not be tolerated. You have any issue, you come to me. Okay?" He stared at the players in front of us, and from my other side I felt Kian, broody and intimidating, his hard gaze daring anyone to have an issue with me.

My teammate Ben caught my eye. "I'm only concerned with the fact that Preston still refers to football as 'soccer.'" He gave me a friendly wink, smiling, and I returned his smile hesitantly. With that, the tension in the room was broken, and I could breathe again.

"Proud of you." Kian's hand brushed over my back in a light, fleeting touch, as he murmured low in my ear. "You okay?" he asked in a slightly louder voice.

"Yeah. Yeah, I am." I was surprised to find that I meant it.

There had been some ribbing, as expected, and I had noticed a few of the guys making a point to stay away from me, particularly in the locker room, but on the whole, I couldn't have asked for more. It was a weight off my mind, and I felt so much lighter. My only regret was that I hadn't said anything sooner.

My phone sounded, Kian's nickname appearing on the screen.

Delinquent: Should I take out my lip ring?
Me: NO. Why would you?
Delinquent: Want to make a good impression
Me: Just be yourself and they'll love you
Delinquent: Is it too late to change my mind?
Me: It's going to be fine. Promise

He didn't reply, but fifteen minutes later, there was a knock at the front door. I'd already instructed my mom to let me answer it, and when I threw it open, I found Kian on the front step, chewing on his lip ring, with a bunch of flowers in fall colours clasped in his hands.

The temperature rose about thirty degrees as I drank him in. Man, he was so damn hot. He'd styled his usually messy hair, and he had on black jeans and a collared deep green shirt that made his eyes look brighter and even more striking than usual, fringed by his dark lashes.

I swallowed hard, willing my dick not to react to him, because...my parents were here.

"Aww, you brought me flowers," I teased, because if I didn't do something to break the tension, I was likely to maul him in the hallway.

"Funny." His tone was dry, but I could hear the shake in his voice that he was trying to hide. My stomach did that flipping thing that it kept doing when he was around, and I moved closer.

"I'm trying to get my mind off the fact that I want to

get you naked, right here with my mom and dad in the next room." I trailed my lips across his ear, and he shuddered.

"You'd better stop that right now, Golden Boy. I can't meet your parents with a hard-on."

I heard the desperation in his voice, and I winced. "Sorry. You drive me crazy. The way you look right now..." Composing myself, I took a conscious step back and met his eyes. "I didn't mean to upset you."

"You didn't." He blew out a heavy breath. "I'm just really fucking nervous, and I want it to go well. I've never met anyone's parents before. I mean, not as the new boyfriend."

"Never?"

He shook his head, and I ran my hand down his arm reassuringly. "I promise they'll love you." We headed into the kitchen, where my mom was putting the finishing touches to the salad she was making to go with the lasagne cooling on the side of the stove. She looked up as we entered, a warm smile spreading across her face.

"You must be Kian." She rounded the counter towards us, and Kian handed her the flowers, giving her a nervous smile that made me step closer to him, needing to reassure him that everything was going to be okay. "Oh, my. Flowers. And such beautiful colours, too." Taking the bouquet, her smile grew wider, and Kian relaxed, his shoulders losing their stiffness.

He licked his lips, then cleared his throat. "Thank you for having me."

Surprising him, she stepped forwards, placing the flowers down and pulling him into a hug. "You're more than welcome. I'm so happy to finally meet the boy my son won't stop talking about."

"Mom." I groaned as she released Kian, before returning her attention to the flowers.

As she shooed us away, I pretended to ignore the smirk he tossed my way as he leaned close to me, lowering his voice. "Won't stop talking about me, hey?"

"Shut up."

He laughed as we took a seat at the kitchen table. My dad came strolling in a moment later, stopping dead when he saw Kian seated at the table with me.

"Kian Courtland, I presume?"

Kian flew out of his seat, spinning to face my dad. "Uh, yes, sir."

My dad laughed, clasping his hand briefly. "No need to be so formal. Call me Mr. M." He grinned at Kian. "I think it may seem a little weird for you to call me Preston, hmm?"

"Dad, please," I groaned. "It's not like he's going to get us mixed up."

Taking a seat across from us, he shot me a wink, before turning back to Kian. "It's good to meet you, son. Preston won't stop talking about you."

"That's what I told him," my mom shouted from the stove, and I buried my face in my hands.

"Can you two please stop embarrassing me?"

Kian joined in the laughter, and I raised my head to find his green eyes sparkling with amusement as he looked at me. I shrugged off my embarrassment. If he was happy, then that was all that mattered to me.

After that, it was easy. My dad got Kian talking about soccer, and we fell into a light-hearted discussion about the US international team's performance in a recent friendly game. As we ate, my mom peppered Kian with anecdotes about my time growing up, and he drank all the information in with a permanent grin on his face.

Once dinner was over and my mom and dad were settled in front of the TV, we finally escaped to my room. My parents were cool with me having my boyfriend in my bedroom, although I wouldn't put it past my mom to drop in unannounced.

Kian threw himself onto my bed, and I lay next to him, content to have him here. "That wasn't so bad, was it?" I trailed my fingers up his arm.

"Your parents are great." A wistful look came into his eyes, and I knew he was thinking about his own parents.

"*You're* great. They loved you." Leaning forwards, I nipped at his jaw.

"You're lucky to have them." His voice was quiet, and he rolled over, burying his face in the crook of his elbow.

"Kian..." I ran my hand over his back, his body tense underneath my palm.

"Why don't they want to know me?"

The pain in his voice cut me deep. "Come here." He shifted so he was lying half across me, half on the bed, his leg draped over mine and his face buried in the crook of my neck. "Listen to me, right now." When he raised his head, shifting so we were level, I reached up and grasped his chin, running my thumb over his light stubble. "You're awesome. You make me..." Unable to articulate exactly how he made me feel, I simply said, "They're idiots."

"Yeah." He sighed, then lowered his head to mine. "Thanks."

Before he could kiss me, I slid out from under him and headed over to my door, flipping the lock. Kian rolled onto his back, staring at me, his eyes darkening as I rejoined him, crawling up his body. "Remember what I said earlier?" I grasped the hem of his shirt, pushing it up to reveal the ridges of his abs.

"That you wanted to get me naked?" He raised a brow, smirking, but his voice was hoarse as he stared down at me.

"Yeah." I flicked open the button of his jeans. "We'll have to be careful, and I can't get you naked like I want, but..." My hand lowered. "Think you can keep quiet when I do this?" Easing his jeans and boxers down, I grasped his thick, hard length in my hand, running my thumb over the precum at the tip. His hips bowed off the bed, and he threw his hand over his mouth, muffling his groan. Leaning back, I undid my own jeans, freeing my cock and running my hand up and down the length.

"Get over here." Lifting his hand, he reached for me.

"Mmm. I like your thinking." As I lined my body up with his, I claimed his mouth in a deep kiss, rolling my hips to create more friction between us.

With a gasp, he arched up off the bed, gripping my ass and moving his hips against mine, swallowing my moans with his mouth. "Preston." His gaze was heavy lidded, his lips swollen from our kisses. "This feels so good."

I tugged his lower lip between my teeth, before releasing it and moving my mouth to his ear. "You—"

"Preston! Cake?"

"Fuck!" Kian bucked me off, frantically pulling up his jeans as my mom's voice sounded from the bottom of the stairs. I couldn't help laughing at his panicked expression even as I raced to pull up my own jeans.

"Cockblocked by your parents." Slightly calmer now we were both clothed, Kian sat up on my bed, shaking his head at me.

Leaning forwards, I ran a hand through his dishevelled hair and placed a kiss to his cheek. "I'm happy that I got to introduce you to them at last, but there are definitely some disadvantages."

He lunged forwards to nip at my jaw, sending us tumbling backwards onto the bed, him on top of me. "You can make it up to me when we're alone."

"I'll more than make it up to you," I promised, as he trailed kisses across my face, pressing his hips into mine.

"Kian. You're killing me." My arms tightened around his body. All I wanted was to lose myself in him.

But I couldn't. Not now.

Reluctantly, we broke apart, taking a moment to adjust ourselves and straighten our clothes, to try and make it look less obvious that we'd been messing around on my bed together. I held out my hand to him. "Come on. Let's go back downstairs, since we can't be trusted to be alone together without me wanting to jump on you. I think we have chocolate cake?"

Taking my hand, he leaned into me, giving me one final kiss before I unlocked and opened the door.

"It's a poor substitute for your cock, but I guess it'll do for now."

I laughed, tugging him out of the room. Pausing at the top of the stairs, I turned to him, meeting his gaze. "You know I want you for more than just your body, right?"

A crooked smile lifted the corners of his lips. "I know. Same." He squeezed my hand. "Come on. Feed me cake and tell me more about your life growing up in the US. I want to know everything."

"Deal."

FOURTEEN

KIAN

DECEMBER

"Dad?" I stopped dead in the kitchen, seeing him sitting at the table, studying the newspaper in front of him, a mug of coffee in his hand. "What are you doing here?"

"I live here." He spoke brusquely without even bothering to look up from his paper. *Yeah, but you're never here* was on the tip of my tongue, but I swallowed the words. Setting his coffee down, he turned the page of his newspaper. "No more temper tantrums lately. I'm almost disappointed in you." Now his eyes flicked to mine as his harsh words taunted me.

I balled my fists at my side, and I noticed his own were clenched, white-knuckled against the table. He hadn't hit me since I discovered an aptitude for fighting and fought back against him when I was fifteen, but I knew the urge was always there. The asshole disliked the fact I existed, and as far as he was concerned, out of sight was out of mind.

Instead of replying, I turned to walk out of the kitchen,

when his voice stopped me in my tracks. "I trust you're over your little experiment."

Spinning round to look at him, I counted to five in my head before I replied. "What experiment?"

"The *boyfriend*." He spoke the words with distaste. This was the first time I'd spoken to my dad in person since Fright Night, and he wasn't even bringing up the fact that Preston and I had smashed the fuck out of his Bentley. No, all he was concerned with was my relationship with Preston.

"Sorry to disappoint. He's still around."

His eyes narrowed. "He's not welcome in my house. When will you come to your senses and get over this little phase?"

The only thing stopping me from raising my own fists to him was the thought of Preston. "I'm bisexual, Dad. It's not a fucking *phase*." Gritting my teeth, I spun on my heel and left him fuming behind me.

The only person I needed right now was my boyfriend. It was our joint party tonight, but it was still early, and I needed to see him. Stalking through the house and into the garage, I threw open my car door and slid inside.

Fuck. I slammed my hand down on the steering wheel. Dragging my phone from my pocket, I texted Preston.

Me: Need you
Golden Boy: What's up?
Me: My dad
Golden Boy: Meet at the warehouse? I'll leave now
Me: I'll pick you up
Golden Boy: OK. Hold on. I got you

Without wasting any more time, I gunned the engine and roared out of the garage and away from the house, towards the only person I wanted to see.

The large warehouse owned by our mate Mack provided the backdrop for what was proving to be an epic party. Smoke pumped around the cavernous interior, neon lights pulsed in time to the music, and the DJ worked the crowd into a frenzy. Out the back, we'd set up a chill-out zone—a shipping container we'd filled with seating and dim lighting, and a paint run where people tried to avoid getting hit by paint bombs as they ran through the course. Mack's idea, rather than mine, but I'd taken the credit.

Bottle of beer dangling from my fingers, I leaned against the wall of the shipping container, my eyes on Preston as he made his way over to me with a tray of paint in his hand. We'd been in here for a while, but most of our friends had disappeared now, back in the warehouse either dancing or running around in LED masks, pelting unsuspecting people with paint bombs.

As he reached me, he leaned in close, his eyes dark in the dim lighting. "Ready for me to mark you?" He'd been decorating faces and even bodies for half the evening, smearing neon colours across skin, while I'd watched him, mesmerised, unable to tear my gaze away.

I nodded, placing my drink on the upturned crate next to me. He dipped his fingers into the paint, and then he brought his hand up to my face. Shivers raced down my body as he dragged his paint-covered fingers across my skin, slowly and surely.

Preston had an effect on me that I wasn't even sure I

understood. When I'd shown up at his house, pissed off and upset, he seemed to instinctively know how to handle me, letting me work through my fucked-up mess of emotions until I was calm. And the physical effect he had on me... there was a reason why I'd been trying not to stay too close to him this evening. I wanted him all the time.

Standing with him here right in front of me, his gaze focused as he drew careful lines across my face, the urge was becoming harder to ignore.

"Done. You look..." He paused, raking his gaze over me as I stared at him, hungry. "Like a delinquent. *My* delinquent."

"Want me to do you?" Swiping my fingers through the paint he was still holding, I leaned closer to him.

"Oh, I want you to do me." His voice was low and seductive. My dick strained against my jeans.

"I..." Licking my suddenly dry lips, I tried again. Preston's eyes followed my movements, his body so close to mine that I could feel the heat radiating from him. "Fuck it," I muttered, wiping the paint on my jeans. "Let's get out of here."

He laughed as I pushed away from the wall, heading for the exit as fast as I could. "Wanna try the paint run?" he murmured low in my ear, as we exited the container. This close, it took all my willpower not to turn my head and close the gap between us, to claim him as mine.

When would I be ready to do that? I'd come out to my dad, and Preston's parents knew; why was it so hard to do the same with my friends?

I shook the thought off for now. "The paint run? *Not* what I had in mind."

A low chuckle escaped him. "I know. I know what you

want." Moving past me, he ducked around the corner of the warehouse. "This way."

When I reached him, leaning against the warehouse wall, hidden by the corner of the container, he tugged me into him, burying his face in my shoulder, before drawing back to look at me.

My hand went to his hair, running my fingers through the soft strands and down to clasp the back of his neck. "I missed you so fucking much." I rested my forehead against his, staring into his blue eyes. "I've been wanting to touch you all night."

"I know. Me too." He pressed his lips to mine, before drawing back.

His words sent a spike of guilt straight to my gut.

He seemed to know what I was thinking because he ran his hands up and down my back in reassuring strokes. "Hey. I'm not trying to give you a guilt trip."

I nodded. There'd never been any pressure from him, just never-ending patience as he let me come to terms with everything in my own time. "I know. Sorry, it's..."

"Don't apologise."

"I—"

He shut me up effectively by lunging at me and slamming his mouth down on mine. Everything else was forgotten as our lips collided in a bruising kiss.

Fuuuuck.

I gripped his ass, pulling his hips into me, kissing him harder, our teeth clashing as we fought for dominance. My hand went to his jeans, undoing them and yanking them down, and he reciprocated by doing the same, before grinding against me again. Through the thin barrier of our underwear, my cock rubbed against his in a way that was both hot as fuck and insanely frustrating, because all we had was this stolen moment around the back of the container.

"Kian..." Preston's voice trailed off as I went for his neck, sucking at his warm skin. Maybe I wasn't ready to tell people about us yet, but in the meantime, I was going to mark him as mine.

A curse fell from his lips when I dragged my teeth across his throat, and he pushed down my boxers, before shoving his own down. "Spit," he commanded, his palm by my mouth. Then, his hands were grasping both our cocks. "Hands on the wall. Now." He bit my jaw, his teeth scraping against my stubble, thrusting his hips towards me.

"So controlling," I rasped, my hands going to the cold bricks either side of his head almost of their own accord. I felt the wall vibrate under my palms, the heavy bass of the music from inside the warehouse reverberating through the entire space and permeating our dark corner.

"You love it." He left bites across my jaw, before pulling my lip between his teeth.

Yeah, I did. And so did my cock, so hard against his, leaking precum over his fingers as he moved his hands in a rhythm that was driving both of us insane. "Feels so good," I panted, and he responded with a low moan of agreement. My lips found his, crushing our mouths together in another bruising kiss, as his movements became faster, harder, both of us racing towards the edge.

"I'm gonna come." My voice was barely recognisable, thick with lust, as my balls tightened, and hot cum covered his hands.

"Oh, fuck." He stiffened against my body, shuddering against me, his head dropping to my shoulder. I lowered my arms from the wall, winding them around his broad shoulders as I held him. When we'd both managed to catch our breath, he raised his head and gave me one of his soft smiles that he never seemed to direct at anyone else. Smiles that made me feel things I'd never felt before. "You okay?"

Leaning forwards, I brushed my lips over his. "Never better."

He smiled against my mouth, before a shiver went through his body. "It's kinda cold out here, huh?"

Yeah, it was. It was winter, after all. "What, my body isn't enough to keep you warm?" I pressed against him, and he huffed out a laugh, burying his face in my shoulder and hugging me tightly. Keeping one arm around him, I lifted my hand and ran my fingers through his hair. "Let's clean up and I'll warm you up by chasing you around the paint run."

"Or I could chase you," he suggested, raising his head.

"You already caught me, remember."

"Yeah. I caught myself a delinquent." His lips curved into a teasing grin, and I knew we were both thinking of the words he'd said to me on Fright Night. "It was the mask, wasn't it? That was how I managed to get close to you without you knowing it was me."

I made a point of looking him up and down. "Nah, there's no disguising you. Even with that mask. Guess you just got lucky."

"Mmm. I did."

My eyes met his. "So did I. I'm glad you caught me," I said hoarsely.

His arms tightened around me as he held my gaze. "Me too."

FIFTEEN

PRESTON

Kian's first day back training with the soccer team, and it wasn't going well. Coach was riding us hard, and our team captain was in a dark mood, affecting everyone. When Coach blew the whistle for a break, I headed over to Kian, pulling him aside for a brief moment. "Why don't you go and talk to Carter, see what's up?"

Kian nodded, breathing hard. "Yeah, I'm going to speak to him now." He jogged off in the direction of Carter, and I headed over to the side of the field, picking up a bottle of water and uncapping it. Out of the corner of my eye, I could see Kian and Carter, deep in discussion. Man, I wanted to be over there with him. As much as I didn't want to put any pressure on him, and wouldn't, I wanted to have our relationship out in the open. I'd never felt this way about anyone before, and I wanted everyone to know that this amazing guy was all mine.

With a sigh, I tore my gaze away from Kian and dropped into a series of stretches, working out my aching muscles. My teammates were doing the same around me or lying collapsed in the grass.

As I started stretching out my hamstrings, my gaze swung back to Kian. He was looking at me, and right then, all his usual walls that he had up around our friends were down. He was looking at me the way he did when we were alone.

My heart beat faster.

He beckoned me over to where he stood with Carter, and I jogged slowly over to them, my legs shaky. As soon as I reached them, Kian threw his arm around my waist and kissed me, hard and desperate.

What the fuck?

Caught off guard, I stumbled back, but Kian steadied me. I studied him closely, seeing nothing but pure determination in his eyes. A smile spread across my face as I held his gaze. He'd just kissed me in front of the entire soccer team, and it hadn't gone unnoticed.

He'd outed himself. For me. For *us*.

"I take it the secret's out?" I managed, when my brain finally wrapped itself around the fact that Kian had come out. To *all* our teammates. His closest friends.

Carter's stunned expression faded, and he gave us a genuine smile. "I'm happy for you both. How long has this been going on?"

"Since Fright Night," Kian told him, tightening his hold on my waist. I leaned into him, because I could. The smile wouldn't leave my face.

"I wasn't the only one to have a secret hook-up over Halloween, then." Carter grinned at Kian. Before I could ask him about that, we were interrupted by the whistle blowing again, and we headed back onto the field.

Everything was different now. Whatever Kian had said to Carter had impacted his mood for the better, and as for me, I was walking on air after Kian's public claiming. The team came together, working as one well-oiled machine, and the passes between me and Kian were effortless. I felt high, able to conquer the world.

When practice ended and we'd finished our cool-down stretches, I pulled Kian aside as the rest of the team made their way back to the locker room. He was covered in mud, sweating, and still breathing hard, but to me, he'd never looked better.

"Are you sure about this?" Running my hand through my hair, I stared at him.

His reply was instant. "Yeah. I should've done it sooner. Way sooner." He gave me a crooked smile, stepping closer and putting his arms around me. "You're pretty fucking special to me, Golden Boy, and it's about time people around here were aware of just who you belong to."

It took me a while to formulate a reply, the lump in my throat too big to swallow around. I lowered my forehead to his, my arms sliding around his waist. "You're everything to me."

His grip on me tightened, and he blew out a heavy breath. We stayed like that for a moment, just enjoying the closeness between us, before he released me. "I feel like a weight's been lifted, y'know?"

"I know." I turned in the direction of the locker rooms. "I'm proud of you. And happy. You make me so happy, Kian."

His eyes shining, he took my hand and squeezed it lightly, before tugging me towards the locker rooms.

"So this is how we celebrate making things properly official, huh?" Smiling, I looked down at Kian's hand clasped around mine, as we came to a stop at the end of the boardwalk that stretched out over the sea.

"Maybe I'm trying to romance you before I take you back to mine and do bad things to you." He shrugged, a grin playing across his lips.

"Oh, baby, you're so sweet." I pretended to swoon, batting my lashes at him, and he hit me in the bicep. I glared at him. "Hey! That was uncalled for."

"You're a dick," he said, laughing. "Good thing I like you so much."

"Says the guy who just punched me."

We grinned at each other, and I savoured being out here in the open with my boyfriend. No more hiding away, no more having to walk next to him without being able to hold his hand. Now, everyone could see that he was mine and I was his.

"Is this okay for you, being with me, in the open? Do you feel uncomfortable?" I ran my hand down his arm, feeling his hard muscles flex under my touch.

He took an unsteady breath. "It feels...new. But good. Really good." Taking a step closer, he grasped my chin in his hand, running his thumb over my jaw. "I have no regrets about any of this. I promise."

"Good. But I want you to tell me if you ever feel uncomfortable, okay?"

In response, he nodded and lightly nipped at my lower lip. "Speaking of romancing you..." A flush appeared on his cheeks, and he shuffled his feet. "Do you want to go out with me? For a meal or something?"

A wide smile spread across my face. "Are you asking me on a date?"

"Yeah. I know we've probably done things the wrong way round...okay, we definitely have, but I want you to know that you're important to me. I want to be seen with you. Would that be alright?"

"Hell, yeah. It's more than alright. I'd love to."

He smiled back at me, his eyes sparkling, and I kissed him.

We fell silent, his arm against mine as we leaned against the railing. I breathed in the salty tang of the sea air, memories of my home on the Connecticut coast flooding back as I stared out to sea.

"Do you miss it?"

Kian's voice broke through my thoughts, and I turned to see him studying me intently from under his lashes, his dark hair windswept from the sea breeze. Damn, he was gorgeous. How did I get so lucky?

"Huh?"

"America," he elaborated. "You've got that distant look in your eyes, like you get when you're thinking about it."

"You noticed that?" I stared at him in surprise, and he gave me a small smile.

"Yeah. I dunno if you're aware, but I notice a lot about you, Golden Boy."

My heart skipped a beat. I cleared my throat before replying. "Me too." He gave me a soft smile, which didn't mask the question in his eyes, and I gave him my full attention, turning to lean sideways on the railing so I could face him properly. "I do miss it. Sometimes it's like a physical pain, an ache deep inside. It's...it's my homeland."

A sadness stole over his face that he tried to conceal with a smile that didn't reach his eyes. I tugged him into my arms. "You know what, though?" I waited until he looked at me, and I continued, telling him my truth. "I'm happier now than I ever have been."

"Yeah?" His voice was a croaky whisper.

"Yeah. Sure, it hasn't been easy, but I've gained more than I've lost. I got you, didn't I?"

This time, his smile reached his eyes. "True."

"Not only that, but now we're official, I can take you back to my hometown one day. Show off the hot British bad boy I managed to charm into being my boyfriend."

He pulled me closer, his voice a husky murmur against my lips. "I'd like that."

SIXTEEN

KIAN

JANUARY

We were on fire. That was the only way to describe us. Or, in the words of the local press, who must've been having a quiet week because they'd been hyping my return to the team way more than was necessary:

> *Could there be a better pairing? Watch out for Kian Courtland and Preston Montgomery III, the star strikers of Alstone High's football team. With this dynamic duo reigning as an unstoppable force on the pitch, and the experience and intuition of Carter Blackthorne at the helm, the coveted championship trophy is well within Alstone High's grasp.*

I wasn't complaining, though. I was fucking good at what I did, and it had only been my stupidity that had got me suspended in the first place. Now, I was back where I belonged.

This game was important for so many reasons, the first

and foremost being that it was the quarter-finals of the championships, and we were playing our biggest rivals, Highnam Academy. It was my first game back, and I soaked up the atmosphere, reacting to the roars of the crowd, my heartbeat pounding loud in my ears as I passed the ball back and forth to my teammates, intercepting the Highnam defenders and claiming possession of the ball. Flying down the field, my eyes scanning for any openings I could take, my feet knew what to do before my brain could catch up.

Carter passed me the ball, and my foot flew out, sending it straight to Preston. Highnam didn't have a hope of intercepting that pass, and they knew it. Preston's foot connected with the ball, and he sent it straight into the goal.

The stadium went mad, and I ran for him, jumping onto his back and fist pumping the air with one hand while my other gripped him around his neck. He laughed, holding on to my thighs as the crowd roared around us. The euphoria of scoring a goal and being here with him fizzed through my blood.

"I love you!" I shouted the words in his ear, and he froze beneath me. Sliding off his back, I pulled him into a hug, as our teammates piled on us, celebrating the goal. His eyes found mine in the midst of it all, a question in them, and I mouthed the words to him again.

I love you.

A bright, beaming smile lit up my golden boy's face, before he was being tugged away from me, and we were back in the game.

There was no time to talk, and maybe I should've waited to tell him, maybe there was a better setting than in the middle of our biggest football game of the season so far, but I couldn't hold it in any longer. He needed to know how I felt about him.

I loved him.

He was my entire world.

At half-time, I jogged off the pitch with the rest of the team, and Preston caught up with me as we entered the changing rooms, where our coach was waiting to talk to us. "Did you mean what you said?" His voice was low next to my ear.

"Yeah, I meant it, Golden Boy." I hooked my finger around his, before releasing it and taking a seat on the benches. I felt his gaze on mine, and I turned to catch his eye, throwing him a wink. He stared at me, happiness radiating from him, and my heart stuttered. *I'd* managed to do that. Managed to put that huge smile on his face, to make him the happiest I'd ever seen him. He opened his mouth to say something, but the coach began speaking and we both turned our attention to him.

There'd be time to talk afterwards. Right now, we had a football match to win.

As soon as we hit the football pitch and the whistle blew, Highnam Academy were all over us, muscling through our defence line and scoring a goal. Carter held the team together, refusing to let us falter, and we rallied, working as one to block their constant attacks, while still creating our own chances. The end of the game drew closer with no further goals from either team, both of us too evenly matched.

Out of the corner of my eye, I saw my teammate Chris get taken down by a foul. Carter looked over at me, and I nodded. We were already into added time, and this was our last chance. He took up position on the sideline and booted the ball in a curving arc, over the heads of the Highnam players. I leapt into the air, my head connecting with the ball, and I sent it straight into the back of the net.

The roar of the crowd was deafening. My teammates piled onto me, shouting and cheering as we celebrated, knowing there was no chance Highnam would be able to score now. And less than a minute later, the whistle sounded to mark the end of the match.

We'd won.

I was grabbed from behind and spun around, Preston's mouth coming down hard on mine. Twisting my arms around him, I spread my hands across his shoulders, loving the feel of his muscles under my palms. He growled, kissing me harder, before pulling back, both of us trying to catch our breath.

His sapphire eyes met mine.

"I love you, Kian."

I nipped at his lip, and he reciprocated, clasping my face in his hands, before dragging his tongue across my lip piercing. Lunging forwards, I kissed him again, before drawing back. "Preston." My forehead rested against his. "I love you so fucking much. This isn't the time or the place for what I want to do to you, but what do you say we get showered and go celebrate somewhere more private?"

"Yes. Please."

Clasping his hand, I led him off the pitch.

PRESTON

EPILOGUE

THREE MONTHS LATER

"Back where it all began, huh? The first time I had you?" Kian backed me against the shower wall, his hands running down my chest, grinding his hard length against mine. We normally spent time alone at his house, since his parents were never around, but mine had flown back to the US for a visit and I planned to make the most of our night together. Kian and I would be joining them tomorrow for the latter part of their trip, but for tonight, we were all alone.

"Mmm. The first time you had me was technically in my bed." My words ended on a groan, as he reached down between us to encircle both of our cocks, running his teeth along my jaw as the water rained down on his back.

"Details," he panted, moving his hand faster. "Fuck, your cock feels so good against mine."

My balls tightened as I spiralled closer to the edge, my head falling forwards to his shoulder, where I sank my teeth into him. Abruptly, he stopped and turned around in my arms, pushing backwards so my cock slid against his ass, making me stifle a groan.

"I want you." Turning his head, he nipped at my jaw, and I ground against him as he reached his arm behind him to grip my ass, pulling me closer. "I want you to fuck me." His voice was low and determined.

My mouth opened and closed a few times. We'd experimented with fingers, which, yeah, he'd become a big fan of, especially when I sucked his cock at the same time, but as far as anything else went, he'd only said that he wanted to work up to it. I'd never forced the situation. "Really? Are you sure?"

"Yeah." He hesitated. "Unless...do you have a preference?"

I dropped my head to his shoulder and kissed his wet skin. "Not really. Before y—"

In an instant, his hesitation was gone, and he growled, spinning around and pushing me back against the wall, his green eyes flashing. "There's no *before*. Only *me*."

"Damn, Kian. You're so sexy when you get all possessive." Gripping his ass, I yanked him into me, kissing him hard. Our teeth collided, tongues lashing, water raining down on both of us as we rebounded off the wall of the wet room.

"Fuck. Me. Right. Now." Kian tore his mouth away, panting out the words, his eyes darkened to black as he stared at me, the water droplets clinging to his eyelashes and hair.

"Yes."

Lying back on the bed, I drank in the sight of Preston lowering his head between my thighs, his lube-coated fingers gliding down to my ass. He paused, his mouth so close that I could feel his breath across the head of my cock, and looked up at me from beneath his lashes.

"If at any point you want me to stop, tell me, okay?"

I stared down at him. "I don't want you to stop. If you don't get your mouth on my cock in the next—"

My golden boy gave me the filthiest grin I'd ever seen, then enveloped my cock in his hot mouth, making me gasp. "Fuuuuck, yes." My hips jerked up as I threw my head back, gripping onto his hair.

Working his fingers carefully into me, one at a time, he licked and sucked my erection, alternating the pace and pressure until I was thrusting up into his mouth, desperate for release. The pressure of his fingers inside me was so fucking good, but I needed *more.*

"Need your cock," I rasped, tugging at his hair. "I'm gonna come before you get inside me."

He raised his head and licked his swollen lips, his eyes heavy-lidded as he met my gaze. Raising himself up over my body, he slowly withdrew his fingers and lowered his head to flick his tongue across my lip ring. "Can I have you like this? I want to see your face."

"However the fuck you want. Need you now." My voice was thick with lust, the friction of his body against mine driving me wild. I'd wanted him like this for so long, it would kill me to wait any longer.

Going up onto his knees, he ran his hands down my thighs, before positioning me so my knees were bent with my legs up. "If you could see yourself right now..." He rolled on a condom, liberally covering it with lube, before sliding it across my hole. "I'm gonna go slow. Relax, okay?"

Then the head of his cock was at my entrance, and my breath caught in my throat as he began to move. There was a pressure as he pushed inside in slow increments, his muscles tensing as he held himself back from thrusting all the way in.

"Breathe," he instructed me in a low voice. "You're incredible. I love you so much."

I breathed, trying to relax myself, but fuck, he was so big. Fingers hadn't prepared me for the stretch and burn as he eased inside me.

"Breathe," he repeated, keeping his eyes on mine. "You doing okay?"

"It...I'm gonna feel it tomorrow, but don't stop."

"You feel so good." He gripped my cock, palming the length until I was fully hard and throbbing beneath his hand. "*Kian.*" His nostrils flared as he looked down between us. "You-you..."

"Speechless, huh?" I attempted a smirk, but fuck, I was so lost in him. The look in his eyes, the feeling of fullness as he sank balls-deep into me, his hand on my cock. "I love you." Reaching up, I pulled his head down to mine, kissing, biting, touching, and he responded while his lower body remained still, allowing me to get used to the feel of him inside me.

He kissed me harder, more desperately, but rolled his hips in a slow, careful movement.

"Don't hold back," I gasped, tearing my mouth from his. "Fuck me. Hard." Reaching down, I gripped his ass, pulling him closer so there was no space between us. "I want to feel you so fucking deep that I can't sit down tomorrow."

I felt him shudder as he raised his body. "I can do that." He swallowed thickly, then thrust his hips forwards. And again. And again. Then, he moved, changing the angle, and *fuuuuck.*

"More" was all I managed, as he nailed me in just the right place, the sensation almost unbearably good.

"So. Good," he groaned, staring down at me with his pupils completely blown, as he pushed us both closer and closer to the edge. I clenched around him, and he pulsed inside me, his breath unsteady as he shook against my body. His hand jerked on my cock, and I moved my hand to join his, my cum shooting over both of our stomachs as he collapsed on top of me.

Running my fingers through his hair, still fucking shaking and breathless, I finally managed to regulate my breathing. He pressed closer to me, burying his face in my shoulder. "Fuck, man. I never. You. *Kian.*"

I tugged his head up so our lips could meet.

No more words were needed.

The lights of JFK Airport glittered below us as the plane circled, moving lower in the sky as we drew closer to our destination. Preston gripped my hand, both of us craning our necks to watch the view below through the tiny plane window.

"Once we hit the road, it should only take us around an hour or so to get to my aunt's house." Preston repeated the information he'd already told me at least six times, but the excitement in his voice was contagious and I couldn't help grinning.

I only had to turn my head slightly to line my mouth up with his ear. "Have I ever told you how much I love you?"

He shivered as I tugged his earlobe between my teeth, before releasing it. "Yeah, but I don't mind you telling me again." Our eyes met, and his humour died away. "I love you, too. So much." Bringing his free hand to my face, he ran his thumb across my mouth, brushing over my lip ring, before he leaned forwards and kissed me softly.

His gaze returned to the window, drinking in his homeland, growing closer and closer beneath us.

As the plane taxied down the runway and came to a halt, he turned and smiled at me, his eyes shining brightly.

"Welcome to the USA. I can't wait to show you everything."

THE END

THANK YOU

Thank you so much for reading Kian and Preston's story!

Feel free to send me your thoughts, and reviews are always very appreciated!

Do you want more from Alstone High? Get Trick Me Twice (M/F) and Savage Rivals (M/M) now, available in Kindle Unlimited and paperback. Both books are standalone. Find the links below:

Trick Me Twice (M/F): http://mybook.to/tmt
Savage Rivals (M/M): http://mybook.to/savagerivals

Becca

xoxo

THANK YOU

ACKNOWLEDGMENTS

Originally, Kian and Preston were supposed to be side characters in Trick Me Twice. Somehow, they ended up with their own short story in an anthology, and they wouldn't leave me alone until I told the rest of their story - hence this novella. I fell in love with these two, and I'm so happy I told their story.

Sandra, thank you for editing this on the tightest deadline ever, and Cassie for blowing me away with another awesome cover in a similarly short amount of time! And Sid, proofreading queen!

So much of this story was a team effort. Thank you to Claudia and Jenny for encouraging me to write this, even though it wasn't planned. Thanks to my reader group, Becca's Book Bar, for coming up with amazing title suggestions, and to Courtney for coming up with the final title of Cross the Line. Beta queens Ashley, Bibi, Claudia, Jenny, Megan and Sue, thank you for all your valuable input. Once again, my ST and ARC readers - thank you for all you do. Thanks to the bloggers and friends and readers who are always there to support. I appreciate you!

A special thanks goes to Si and Jon. You've inspired me in more ways than you know. This book definitely wouldn't have been possible without you guys. I love you both! (P.S. I dedicated this book to you, which I think means you owe me a bottle of gin.)

And finally, thanks to you, for choosing to read Kian and Preston's story.

Becca xoxo

TRICK ME TWICE

(M/F | HIGH SCHOOL BULLY ROMANCE | STANDALONE)

Keep my head down and make it through my final year of school without attracting any attention. That was my plan.
The thing about plans? They change.
One day, I was an invisible loner, the next, my name was on everyone's lips.
Why?
I caught the attention of the wrong person.
I tricked Carter Blackthorne, the king of Alstone High.
He found out.
And now?
Now, he's making me pay.

It's time for you to pay the price.
You tricked me once, but you won't trick me twice.

Ready or not, here I come...

http://mybook.to/tmt

SAVAGE RIVALS

(M/M | HIGH SCHOOL ENEMIES TO LOVERS ROMANCE | STANDALONE)

Asher Henderson.
Captain of the Highnam Academy football team, and the bane of my existence.
As Alstone High's team captain, I've been pitted against him from the beginning, but our conflict isn't only reserved for the pitch.
Everyone knows we're enemies. From our first encounter, our rivalry has been escalating, spiralling out of control.

Until one night when everything between us changed.
He pushed me too far, and we crossed a line that should never have been crossed.
Now, I can't get him out of my head.
Can we ever be more than rivals, or are there too many obstacles in our way?

One thing I know for sure.
Things between us will never be the same again.

http://mybook.to/savagerivals

ABOUT THE AUTHOR

Becca Steele is a USA Today and Wall Street Journal bestselling romance author. She currently lives in the south of England with a whole horde of characters that reside inside her head.

When she's not writing, you can find her reading or watching Netflix, usually with a glass of wine in hand. Failing that, she'll be online hunting for memes, or wasting time making her 500th Spotify playlist.

Join Becca's Facebook reader group Becca's Book Bar, sign up to her mailing list, or visit her website https://authorbeccasteele.com

Other links:

- facebook.com/authorbeccasteele
- instagram.com/authorbeccasteele
- bookbub.com/authors/becca-steele
- goodreads.com/authorbeccasteele
- amazon.com/Becca-Steele/e/B07WT6GWB2

ALSO BY BECCA STEELE

The Four Series

The Lies We Tell

The Secrets We Hide

The Havoc We Wreak

*A Cavendish Christmas (free short story)**

The Fight In Us

The Bonds We Break

Alstone High Standalones

Trick Me Twice

Cross the Line (M/M)

*In a Week (free short story)**

Savage Rivals (M/M)

London Players Series

The Offer

London Suits Series

The Deal

The Truce

*The Wish (a festive short story)**

Other Standalones

*Mayhem (a Four series spinoff)**

Boneyard Kings Series (with C. Lymari)

Merciless Kings (RH)

Vicious Queen (RH)

Ruthless Kingdom (RH)

**all free short stories and bonus scenes are available from https://authorbeccasteele.com*

Made in United States
Troutdale, OR
07/26/2024